Jokha Alharthi is the author of ten works, including three collections of short fiction, two children's books, and three novels in Arabic. Fluent in English, she completed a PhD in Classical Arabic Poetry in Edinburgh, and teaches at Sultan Qaboos University in Muscat. *Celestial Bodies* was shortlisted for the Sahikh Zayed Award for Young Writers and her 2016 novel *Narinjah* won the Sultan Qaboos Award for culture, art and literature. Her short stories have been published in English, German, Italian, Korean and Serbian.

Marilyn Booth holds the Khalid bin Abdallah Al Saud Chair for the Study of the Contemporary Arab World, Oriental Institute and Magdalen College, Oxford University. In addition to her academic publications, she has translated many works of fiction from the Arabic, most recently *The Penguin's Song* and *No Road to Paradise*, both by Lebanese novelist Hassan Daoud.

CELESTIAL BODIES

Sayyidat al-qamar

JOKHA ALHARTHI

translated
by
MARILYN BOOTH

SIMON &
SCHUSTER

London • New York • Sydney • Toronto • New Delhi

First published in Great Britain by
Sandstone Press Ltd

This paperback edition published by Simon & Schuster India, 2019

First published in the Arabic language as SAYYIDAT AL QAMAR

Cover photograph by Ionela Yammine

9 10

Simon & Schuster India

818, Indraprakash Building,
21, Barakhamba Road,
New Delhi 110001

www.simonandschuster.co.in

Paperback ISBN: 978-93-86797-56-8
eBook ISBN: 978-93-86797-57-5

Printed and bound in India by Replika Press Pvt. Ltd.

Simon & Schuster India is committed to sourcing paper that is made from wood grown in sustainable forests and support the Forest Stewardship Council,® the leading international forest certification organisation. Our books displaying the FSC® logo are printed on FSC® certified paper.

To my mother

Shaykh Sa'id ibn Muhammad
brother of
Masoud ibn Hamad ibn Muhammad

Salima
m. Azzan ibn Mayya

Hilal

Sulayman (the merchant)
m. Fatima

Ishaq

Abdallah's aunt

Issa ibn Shaykh Ali
(the Emigrant)

Najiya bint Shaykha
(Qamar)

Ankabuta (Khayzuran)
m. Nasib

Zarifa
m. Habib

Masouda
m. Zayd

Muhammad
(died as
infant)

Hamad
(died as
child)

Mayya
m. Abdallah ibn
Sulayman

- London 1981
  m. Ahmad
- Salim 1984
- Muhammad 1991

Marwan

Asma
m. Khalid ibn Issa

- Ali
- Ghaliya

Khawla
m. Nasir

Sanjar
m. Shanna

- Rasha

Translator's Introduction

Celestial Bodies is Omani novelist and academic Jokha Alharthi's acclaimed second novel, first published as *Sayyidat al-qamar* (literal translation: 'Ladies of the Moon'). The book traces an Omani family over three generations, shaped by the rapid social changes and consequent shifts in outlook that Oman's populace have experienced across the twentieth century and in particular since Oman's emergence as an oil-rich nation in the 1960s. One of a wave of historical novels that constitutes a major subgenre of fiction in the Arab world, this work is narrated against a carefully evoked historical canvas. As the critic Munir 'Utaybah remarked, 'A complete world of social relations, practices and customary usages is collapsing, sending the novel's characters to the very edge, the border between two worlds, one of them a suffocating, rigid yet now fragile world and the other one mysterious, ambiguous, full of tensions and anxiety, of uneasy surveillance and fear of what will come ... It is a precarious edge between one era and another, the border between the world of masters and that of slaves, between the worlds of human beings and of supernatural *jinn*, between living reality and nightmare, between genuine love and imagined love, between the society's idea of a person and a person's sense of self.'*

At the heart of *Celestial Bodies* is an upper-class Omani family whose members are expected to maintain traditional ways with only a tentative embrace of minimally modified social behaviour. But, trying to control the effects of social change, the family cannot repress an unspoken history of unacceptable liaisons and of master-slave relations. The impact of a strong patriarchal system on both women and subordinate men is unsparing but it shapes different generations, and individuals, distinctly as it leads to both suffering and confrontation. We find a patriarch whose love for a Bedouin woman tears apart his marital relationship. His wife, adhering to the strictures of patriarchy, seeks her own kind of authority through denial of her granddaughter's challenge to inherited values through an unacceptable linkage to a man of lower social status. The older woman herself has had a difficult childhood in her uncle's home.

Three daughters exemplify diverse reactions to the society's notion of ideal womanhood in a time of rapid socioeconomic transition. The eldest, Mayya, prefers not to challenge her family and acquiesces in marriage to the son of a rich merchant. The second daughter, Asma, seeks an education; she marries an artist but one who is a relative and therefore acceptable. The youngest, Khawla, insists on waiting for her cousin who had told her repeatedly during their childhood that she would be his partner. Yet his emigration to Canada stymies her hopes. The younger generation, following a worldwide trend, move from the family village to Muscat, the capital, and their lives are equally turbulent.

The novel's structure is intricate and engaging. Alternate chapters are narrated by an omniscient narrator and one character, Abdallah, the husband of Mayya. Abdallah's father had been no ordinary merchant; his wealth was derived from a slave trade that had continued despite its legal suppression. Abdallah's life is overshadowed by the mysterious death of his mother; raised by his father's slave, Zarifa – the maternal figure in his life – Abdallah seeks emotional contentment with Mayya, but his love for her is not reciprocated. Through this tracing of intimate family relationships, Alharthi tells a gripping story while offering an allegory of Oman's coming-of-age, and indeed of the difficult transitions of societies faced with new opportunities and pressures. The novel has been praised by critics across the Arab world for its fineness of portraiture, its historical depth and subtlety, and its innovative literary structure.

MARILYN BOOTH
Oriental Institute and Magdalen College, University of Oxford

* Munir 'Utayba, '*Sayyidat al-qamar*: Fitnat al-haki wa-alam al-tadhakkur' (*Sayyidat al-qamar*: the allure of storytelling, the pain of remembering), in his *Fi l-sird al-tatbiqi: Qira'at 'arabiyya wa-'alamiyya* (On narration and critical practice: Readings in Arabic and world literature) (Cairo: al-Hay'a al-'amma li-qusur al-thaqafa, 2015).

Mayya

Mayya, forever immersed in her Singer sewing machine, seemed lost to the outside world. Then Mayya lost herself to love: a silent passion, but it sent tremors surging through her slight form, night after night, cresting in waves of tears and sighs. These were moments when she truly believed she would not survive the awful force of her longing to see him.

Her body prostrate, ready for the dawn prayers, she made a whispered oath. By the greatness of God – I want nothing, O Lord, just to see him. I solemnly promise you, Lord, I don't even want him to look my way … I just want to see him. That's all I want.

Her mother hadn't given the matter of love any particular thought, since it never would have occurred to her that pale Mayya, so silent and still, would think about anything in this mundane world beyond her threads and the selvages of her fabrics, or that she would hear anything other than the clatter of her sewing machine. Mayya seemed to hardly shift position throughout the day, or even halfway into the night, her form perched quietly on the narrow, straight-backed wood chair in front of the black sewing machine with the image of a butterfly on its side. She barely even lifted her head, unless she needed to look as she groped for her scissors or fished another spool of thread out of the plastic sewing basket which always sat in her small wood utility chest. But Mayya heard everything in the world there was to hear. She noticed the brilliant hues life could have, however motionless her body might be. Her mother was grateful that Mayya's appetite was so meagre (even if, now and then, she felt vestiges of guilt). She hoped fervently, though she would never have put her hope into words, that one of these days someone would come along who respected Mayya's talents as a seamstress as much as he might appreciate her abstemious ways. The someone she envisioned would give Mayya a fine wedding procession after which he would take her home with all due ceremony and regard.

That someone arrived.

As usual Mayya was seated on that narrow chair, bent over the sewing machine at the far end of the long sitting room that opened onto the compound's private courtyard. Her mother walked over to her, beaming. She pressed her hand gently into her daughter's shoulder.

Mayya, my dear! The son of Merchant Sulayman has asked for your hand.

Spasms shot through Mayya's body. Her mother's hand suddenly felt unbearably heavy on her shoulder and her throat went dry. She couldn't stop imagining her sewing thread winding itself around her neck like a hangman's noose.

Her mother smiled. I thought you were too old by now to put on such a girlish show! You needn't act so bashful, Mayya.

And that was that. The subject was closed and no one raised it again. Mayya's mother busied herself assembling the wedding clothes, concocting just the right blends of incense, having all the large seat-cushions reupholstered, and getting word out to the entire family. Mayya's sisters kept their views to themselves and her father left the matter in her mother's hands. After all, these were her girls and marriage was women's business.

Without letting it be known, Mayya stopped praying. Instead she would whisper, Lord, I made a sacred oath in Your name, her voice wavering between submissive and plaintive. I swore to You that I wanted nothing… nothing at all… Only, I said, I wanted to see him. I promised You I wouldn't do anything wrong, I wouldn't say a word about what I felt deep down. I made a vow and I made it to You. So why did You send this boy, this son of Merchant Sulayman, to our house? Are You punishing me for the love I feel? But I never let him know I loved him. I didn't breathe a word of it to my sisters… Why, why did You send Mr Sulayman's son to our house?

Mayya, you mean you would really leave us? Khawla asked teasingly. Mayya didn't answer.

Are you sure you're ready for it? Asma asked, chuckling. Just keep in mind the Bedouin woman's advice to her daughter, those words to the bride we found in that old book stuffed away in the storeroom, you know, on the cupboard shelves where all those ancient books were put. The *Mustatraf*.

It wasn't in the *Mustatraf*, said Mayya.

This annoyed her sister. What do you know about books, anyway? Asma snapped. It was too there. In *al-Mustatraf fi kull fann mustazraf*, the book bound in red leather, the one on the second shelf. *The Novel Parts in the Elegant Lively Arts* – you know the book. The Bedouin woman tells the bride to use plenty of water for washing, and pile lots of kohl onto her eyelids, and to always pay attention to what there is to eat and drink.

Yes, said Mayya, her face as serious as ever and her voice low. And that I should laugh whenever he laughs, and if there are any tears rolling down his cheeks, there had better be some tears rolling down mine. I must be content with whatever makes him happy and—

What's wrong with you, Mayya? Khawla broke in. The nomad woman didn't say all that. She just meant you'd feel happy as long as he's happy and sad when he is sad.

So who feels any sadness when I am sad? Mayya wondered. Her voice was barely audible now, yet the word *sadness* rang out, discordant, to settle uneasily over the sisters.

When Mayya saw Ali bin Khallaf he had just returned empty-handed from years of study in London. It didn't matter to Mayya that he had no diploma: the sight of him electrified her. He was so tall that the fast-moving clouds seemed to graze his head, and so very thin that Mayya's first thought was that she must prop him up with her own body against the wind as it carried those clouds swiftly away. He was the picture of nobility, she thought. He looked so … so saintly. He could not possibly be an ordinary human being who would drop off to sleep after a long day, whose body gave off sweat. Someone, for instance, who could be easily riled and shout angry words at others.

I promise you, Lord, I only want a tiny glimpse of him, only one more time. This is my solemn oath. And she did see him, at the time of the date harvest. He was leaning against a palm tree. In the heat, he had jerked his head forward to shake off his kummah, and now the delicately embroidered headgear sat at his feet. The sight of him brought tears. She only got as far as the top of the narrow cement-lined canal before she broke into sobs, her tears flowing like the irrigation water that ran over the falaj as it cut a path between the palm trees.

Mayya fixed all her thoughts on her beloved's spirit. She mustered every atom in her being and sent the lot marching into his. Then she held her breath. Her heart all but stopped beating under the fierceness of her concentration. Mayya bent her will to the task, orienting her being toward his, facing it, determined to follow wherever it might go. She sent her spirit into the ether, detaching herself completely from the world. Her body convulsed and she could barely keep herself from collapsing as she telegraphed her whole self to him, transmitting it with every gram of energy she could find. Then she waited for a signal, some response from him, any sign at all that would tell her the message had gotten through, somewhere deep inside.

No sign arrived. There was no response.

I swear to you, Lord, I just want to see him, up close. I need to see at least that he's real, that there's sweat on his forehead. Only once more. With his hand pressed against the tree trunk, his mouth working the pit out of a date. I promise you, God, I will not tell anyone about this sea inside of me when the silt rises to choke me. I swear, Lord, I don't want any attention from him – who am I, after all? A girl who doesn't know anything except how to sew. I don't know about books like Asma does and I'm not pretty like Khawla. I swear, Lord, I will wait a whole month, I can stand it and I'll be patient but then please will You let me see him? I promise I won't drop anything I owe to You, not the prayers that are our duty nor the extra ones we sometimes do. I won't have any dreams that might anger You. I swear it, Lord, I do not want to even touch the skin of his hand or the hair on his head. I swear I won't give any of this a thought, not even about wiping the sweat off his forehead when he is standing there, underneath the palm tree …

Mayya cried and cried, and when Merchant Sulayman's son appeared suddenly at their house she abandoned her prayers.

After the wedding, she returned to praying. It had all happened because of her oath, she told herself. This was her recompense. Allah knew that she was not truthful in every word she swore. He was punishing her for her sin.

When, a few months later, she became pregnant, all she could hope was that the birth would be as easy as her mother's childbirths had been. She remembered her mother talking about Mayya's own birth. I was chasing after a chicken in the courtyard because my uncle had shown up unexpectedly in time for the midday meal. Suddenly my body was exploding. It hurt so much I collapsed, right there in the courtyard, and then I couldn't move. Your father went and got the midwife. Her time has come, Sabeekah said the moment she saw me. She helped me inside – I couldn't do anything on my own – and closed the door, and made me stand up. Stand on my own feet. And then she made me stretch both arms high enough to reach that pole fixed into the wall, and I did my best to hold on. But my legs started giving out. Then Sabeekah shouted – may God be forgiving to that woman! – Ya ayb ish-shoom! Shame on you! Will Shaykh Masoud's daughter give birth lying down because she's too weak to stand tall and straight? For shame, girl!

So I stood straight, clinging to the pole, until you slipped out of me, ya Mayya, right into my sirwal. There was room enough for you in those baggy trousers! You almost died, though. If Sabeekah hadn't prised my hands from the pole, and then if she hadn't dragged you out! You would've died with that cord wrapped round your neck. Ayy wAllahi, I wasn't even checked by a doctor, never – no creature ever saw my body, no, not me! These days you all go to the hospitals in Maskad, where those Indian women and those daughters of the Christians see every inch of you. Ayy wAllahi Mayya, I had you, and all your brothers and sisters, standing as tall as a grand mare. God be good to you, Sabeekah. There I was holding tight to the pole with both hands, and she was shouting at me, Ya waylik! If I hear even one little screech you'll be sorry! Every woman brings babies out of her body, and what a scandal you are then, if you so much as whimper! A scandal, and you the daughter of the Shaykh! I didn't say one word, I didn't complain. Anyway all I could've said was, My Lord my Lord my Lord! And to think that these days, women have their babies lying flat on their backs, and the men can hear their screams from the other end of the hospital. There's no longer any shame in the world, ayy wAllahi!

When her belly was so enormously round that she could not sleep, Mayya said to Merchant Sulayman's son, Listen here. I am not going to have this baby in this place with those midwives crowding around me. I want you to take me to Maskad—

He interrupted her. I've told you a thousand times, the name of the city is Muscat, not Maskad.

She went on as if she hadn't heard him. I want to have the baby in the Saada Hospital.

You'd have my child slide out right into the hands of the Christians?

She didn't answer. When her ninth month came, her husband took her to the home of his uncle in the old Muscat neighbourhood of Wadi Aday. In what the missionaries called their Felicity Hospital – the Saada – she had her baby, a scrawny infant. A girl.

Mayya opened her eyes to see her daughter cradled in her mother's arms. She dropped off to sleep and when she opened her eyes again, the girl was sucking at her breast. When Merchant Sulayman's son came to see the newborn, Mayya told him she'd named the baby girl London.

She's exhausted, of course, he thought. She must have no idea what she's saying. The next day Mayya, the baby girl, and her mother left the hospital for his uncle's home. The baby's name was London, she told his relatives. The wife of her husband's uncle made fresh chicken broth, baked her the special wafer-thin bread known to be good for new mothers, and made her drink fenugreek with honey to strengthen her body. She helped Mayya to wash her hands and then sat down next to her bed.

Mayya, my dear girl …

Yes?

The woman patted her gently. Are you still set on giving the baby such an odd name? Does anyone name their daughter *London*? This is the name of a place, my dear, a place that is very far away, in the land of the Christians. We are all very, very surprised! But never mind, we know you are weak and fragile right now, you've just had the baby, of course you're not yourself and you need more time. Do think again about a good name for the girl. Call her after your mother. Call her Salima.

Mayya's mother was in the room, and she wasn't pleased. Laysh ya hibbat ayni! My dear woman, why would you want to name her for me when I'm still alive and now I'm blessed with a grandchild? I suppose you're ready and waiting for me to die? That's why you'd like the little girl to inherit my name? As God's compensation. Oh dear me!

Hastily, the uncle's wife tried to repair her error. God forbid I would ever think that! she babbled. Lots of folks name their children after their parents, when their mother and father are still strong and healthy. May no evil touch you, Salima! So then. Let's see … well, name her Maryam, or Zaynab, or Safiya. Any name but this *London*.

Defiantly Mayya held the baby up in front of her. What's wrong with London? There's a woman in Jaalaan Town whose name is London.

The uncle's wife was running out of patience. You know very well that's not really her name! It's just a nickname, something people call her because her skin is so pale. And this girl, well, really now …

Mayya lowered the baby to her lap. She may not have light skin like the merchant's family does, but she's still the daughter of this family. And her name is London.

Salima took things into her own hands. It was time for her daughter and granddaughter to return to the family home in al-Awafi. After all, a mother must recover in her family's embrace. Every new mother knew the importance of the forty days following childbirth. Mayya would spend it in her mother's home, under her mother's watchful care.

Listen, son, Salima said to her daughter's husband. Abdallah, listen – about your wife, here. She's had her first child and it's a girl. Girls are a blessing. A girl helps her mother and raises her younger brothers and sisters. What we need for this new mother are forty live chickens and a big jar of good pure mountain honey. Plus a pot of samna, the best country butter churned straight from a cow. When London is a week old I'll shave her head and you will make an offering – as much silver as the little one's hair weighs. It'll be enough to buy a sheep, you'll have it slaughtered and you'll give out the meat to the poor.

Salima pronounced every letter in the name London slowly and distinctly. Abdallah's face changed expression but he nodded. He took his small new family and his mother-in-law back to al-Awafi, their hometown.

Abdallah

The airplane hurtled forward, pitching into heavy clouds. I could not get my eyes to close even though I knew it would be hours before we reached Frankfurt. When women were just starting to have their babies in Felicity Hospital in Muscat, those black Singer sewing machines – which everyone called Farrashas because of the butterfly design stamped on their sleek black sides – had not yet reached Oman. So how could it be that Mayya had already been sewing clothes on a Farrasha? Come to think of it, electricity was only available in a few areas. Maybe it wasn't the Felicity, perhaps there were other hospitals already operating when London was born. Yes, of course there were other hospitals. There was Mercy Hospital in Matrah, there was at least that one, and perhaps also the Nahḍa Hospital in Ruwi. So, why did Mayya insist on giving birth in the missionary hospital? I don't remember . . . I can't tie it all together, all these things that happened. Her mother, saying to me, Slaughter a cow for the sake of London, and give the meat away. Bring us twenty live chickens for your wife – she has some recovering to do. She said precisely *twenty*, I remember, and she said the word *twenty* with emphasis – though I was going to bring her thirty chickens, and a ewe as well . . . Then there was my uncle's wife, in the house in Wadi Aday, standing up in the courtyard to scold me at the top of her voice: London? And you agreed to that? Don't you have anything to say about your own daughter's name?

That old house…I don't know if they tore that house down or sold it. After my uncle died I only saw that aunt of mine once or twice. When London graduated from the Medical School at Sultan Qaboos University, she said, Papa, I want a BMW. And when we moved to our new house, Mayya moved the Farrasha into the storage room there. Why did she stop sewing? When did she stop? After Muhammad came along, surely. Right, he was born the same year I inherited Father's business and we moved to Muscat. Mayya was very happy about the move. She didn't want to remain under her mother's control for the rest of her life, she said. And when she had Muhammad she stopped sewing.

I remember Mayya putting on an enormous feast to celebrate our move to the new house in Muscat. She invited all of her friends and she had to spread out a very long tablecloth to hold all of the food. Salim was in elementary school then, and Muhammad seemed a perfectly ordinary nursing baby. Mayya was happy and sparkling that night. After the party she slipped on her dark blue night shirt.

Do you love me, Mayya? I asked her, once everyone else was asleep. She was startled, I could see that. She said nothing and then she laughed. She laughed out loud, and the tone of it irritated me. Where did you pick up these TV-show words? she asked. Or maybe it's the satellite dish out there. It's the Egyptian films, have they eaten up your mind?

Muhammad, trying to stand up on my knees, and then tugging hard at my beard. Mayya slapped him, and he cried. I never dared shave off my beard until after my father died. And when they started literacy classes, Mayya entered the sixth year straight away, since she already knew how to read and write as well as having some basic maths. Mayya, I said to her, Muhammad is still tiny. Go to school when he is older. I want to learn English, she said. That was before we got the dish at home. And surely, when I asked my question – Mayya wearing the dark blue night shirt – when I asked whether she loved me, that dish hadn't appeared yet, and I wasn't following any TV programmes or watching any Egyptian films . . .

Then, my father, declining fast, in the Nahda Hospital. When I stuck my hand out to meet his, he knocked it away. When I marched in his funeral, my knees abandoned me. Muhammad was only a year old then.

And when I asked Mayya, Do you love me? she laughed. She laughed! Loud enough to shatter every wall in the new house. Her laughter . . . the children fled from it.

Mayya never watched TV serials. Salim loved the Mexican serials for a time but eventually they bored him and he threw himself into video games instead. Every time we went to Dubai he bought two or three games.

Mayya's mother saying to me, Mayya's my darling daughter. Abdallah, my son, she's in your care now, and you must take care of her. But don't take her away, don't take her from me, away to Maskad. No one is better at the sewing machine than she is. Mayya doesn't like to eat much, or to talk much, you know, Abdallah . . .

Earlier, much earlier: me, saying to my father, Please, Father! I want to go to Egypt or Iraq, I want to study at university there. He grabbed me by the neck and barked at me. By this beard of mine, I swear you are not leaving Oman. Do you *want* to sink so low? To come back from Egypt or Iraq with your beard shaven off? Smoking and drinking and I don't know what? Is that who you want to be? So instead, immediately after finishing high school I went to work in his business.

It wasn't until after he died that I could move the family to Muscat. Little London was very cute and she had filled out by then. In the village, every afternoon Mayya bathed her in the falaj. Scampering along the canal with its running water always made her laugh. I bought her Heinz baby food and Milupa baby cereals and powdered formula. She was the only child in all of al-Awafi who got such things. I bought them at the canteen and Mayya boasted of having them. But my father still shouted at me, calling me *boy*. I was the father of three children, I was no boy... Going in to see him in there, and he would start at it again, stripping off his dishdasha and his vest. His sparse white chest hair caught the pale sunlight slinking around those heavy curtains closed over the only window. I went over to open them but he shook his finger at me: Iyyaaka, boy! Watch out you don't! So I left them as they were. He went on shouting, in one of those bouts of raving that took over his mind for most of the two years before his death. Boy! Boy! Tie Sanjar up, tie him to the column on the east side of the courtyard, out there, out in front of the house. Anyone who gives that slave water or shade has to answer to me. I knelt down beside him. Father, the government freed the slaves a long time ago, and then Sanjar went to Kuwait. (Every summer London would say, Papa, let's visit Kuwait! But Mayya always rejected the idea: So we're going to get away from this heat by escaping to somewhere hotter?) An Omani married Sanjar's daughter and she came back with him to live in Muscat. When she saw me in the Nahda Hospital, where she worked as a nurse, she recognised me. At the sight of my father, who was very ill by then, her lips contorted.

My father calls out, weakly, his fever-black lips trembling. Tie up that slave, tie up that Sanjar so he won't steal a sack of onions ever again. I remain silent and he waves his cane at me in fury. Boy, can't you hear me? Listen to what I'm telling you – go and punish him, go, it's the only way he won't steal any more.

London playing in the water, which she loved. London was six when Mayya chewed me out one time for leaving her to play in the muddy flow of water for two hours. London will get polio, she warned me. London will be paralyzed. I couldn't sleep for several nights, and I couldn't take my eyes off her tiny feet. But she didn't come to any harm. She went on scampering around like a miniature gazelle.

My father's lips turned black, his eyebrows receded, and the spit flew in all directions from his mouth. Boy – have you tied that thieving slave Sanjar to the eastern column yet? I took his hand and kissed it but he pushed me away. Father, the government freed all of the slaves, and Sanjar … the government, Father. He growled under his breath as though he had finally heard me. What's the government got to do with it? Sanjar is mine, he doesn't belong to the government. The government can't free my slaves. I bought his mama Zarifa for twenty silver thalers! I fed her, when a sack of rice cost a hundred pure good silver coins. Yes, that's right, a hundred. One thaler knocking against the next! Aah, Zarruf, so pretty … soft and gentle, Zarruf, but then you got older. Aah, that one grew vain and cocky! I married her off to Habib and then she produced this thief. What does the government have to do with any of this? My slave, mine. How could he travel anyway, without getting permission from me? How, boy?

When he began to shiver and quake again, the sweat running down his neck and oozing across his chest, I wiped it away with the blue towel which was always hanging on a nail on the door. After he died, that towel of his vanished. Going into his room, crying uncontrollably, knocking against the floor and writhing in my sweat, I would look for the towel but I could never find it. The Farrasha sewing machine vanished too. I never go into the storeroom but I know Mayya is hiding it somewhere in there.

Mayya makes gorgeous meat sambusak. I only like sambusak shaped by her hands. When we moved to the new house she made a huge platter of it along with everything else. Mayya, I said to her, Let the maid help you cook. She was silent. A few months later, she insisted on sending the maid back to her home town, without any warning. But that night the room smelled of perfume, and I could half-see her body through her dark blue chemise, and I asked her, Do you love me, Mayya? And she was silent. And then she laughed.

Laughed! She laughed.

I was the tallest boy in the class. Zarifa tugged the hem of my dishdasha down as hard as she could. I guess she thought maybe it would last awhile longer if she kept pulling it down. Every time she yanked it hard in back, the neckline in front attacked and nearly choked me. How much do you have there, boy? the teacher asked me. I had carefully saved my gift from the holy day. All I had bought was a single sweet dried coconut bar. Half a riyal, I said. The teacher burst out laughing. Laughter looks so disgusting sometimes. When people laugh, they look like monkeys. Their bellies shake and their necks shudder, and worst of all, their yellow teeth display all the decay. How old are you? Ten, or maybe twelve. The teacher, Ustaz Mamduh, laughed again. You don't even know your own age? You're very big for the first grade! But what could I do about that, when the school didn't even open until I was already halfway grown up? The pupils were all making noise. Their dishdashas did not press against their necks like mine did. Ustaz Mamduh, they whined, we don't want Abbuuud to sit in front of us, he's too tall! Abdallah, you're toooo tall! Ustaz Mamduh took my hand and asked in a whisper, his Egyptian accent as broad as ever, Do you have any jelly-sweets for me? I shook my head. Tomorrow, bring some of those jelly-sweets you folks make here, tomorrow, he said. At home, Zarifa shouted at me. Jelly-sweets? Just like that? Not a pen, not a notebook, no, he said *jelly-sweets*? Habib had abandoned her by then, and Sanjar was always fleeing the house. She dedicated her time to cooking and to me.

Mayya – she was always so busy, at first with sewing and the children, and then it was school and her friends, and then, sleep. When I was little I used to smell the fragrance of broth on Zarifa whenever I shoved my head into her chest, trying to go to sleep. Ustaz Mamduh said, Abdallah knows how to write his name and he will be moved to grade three. That's how I came to be in third grade with four others, all of whom could write their names successfully on the blackboard. Or they had brought chunks of dark Omani jelly-sweets for the teacher. As Egyptian as he was, Ustaz Mamduh loved the Omani delicacy.

The clouds fold up. Suddenly through the small airplane window the sky is clear. Abdallah, son of Merchant Sulayman, dozes off for a few moments. As he wakes up he is still half-talking in his sleep. Don't hang me upside down in the well, don't. Please, no! Don't!

London

As the sun came up, Salima suddenly felt a warm sense of contentment, as though the sun were beaming its rays directly onto her heart. She was a grandmother. True, this reddish lump of flesh with the odd name had none of *her* beauty; but after all, the lump was her granddaughter, and one way or another it made her proud. She swept the courtyard and freshened it up with a sprinkling of water across the packed-dirt surface. She dragged the rolled-up red Persian carpet from the storeroom, shook it hard to expel the dust, and unrolled it along the length of the reception room. In the middle room, she took down the elegant china that always sat in the high dormer-like apertures punctuating the thick plaster wall, and rubbed each piece to a shine before carefully setting them back into their niches. She spread out new bedding on the floor for Mayya and the newborn. She didn't summon clumsy Khawla to bake; she preferred to do it herself, for the bread a recovering new mother needed was very special. She mixed together the pure country butter and mountain honey to spread on the bread, and after all of these preparations, she made certain that Mayya ate every last bite on the plate and drank the milk boiled with fenugreek to the last drop. She made coffee laced with cardamom for the occasion and set out a platter of fresh fruit and dates. She arranged two bottles of rose water and a small cup of saffron on a gilt tray with the incense burner, and put the coffee, plates and tray of scents in the room ready for visits from her neighbours. She knew the women would soon come round. She bathed herself in water steeped in her special blend of herbs – since the day she was created soap had never touched her body. She put on her best robe and knelt down beside her silent daughter.

Suddenly a loud, gruff voice filled the entire courtyard. *Bismillahi ... ma sha' allah ... allahumma salli ala n-nabi ... allahumma salli ala l-habib ... bismillahi ...* In the name of God, the One who is merciful and compassionate. May blindness strike the eye of the envious one! Ma sha' allah, it's God's will, this is right! The first one's a girl, and a girl comes to raise her little brothers. Ten boys will follow her, God willing. Bismillahi ... allahuma salli ala n-nabi. Prayers be on the blessed Prophet!

At this voice, Salima gave her daughter a little warning slap. Don't even think about getting yourself up, not for just anyone, girl! Not for her. It's only the old man's sweetheart, that's all.

Zarifa strutted down the long room, pausing deliberately and methodically, the name of God streaming incessantly from her mouth. She dug her toes energetically into the Persian carpet to test its depth and softness. She shoved aside the thin, almost transparent cloth that protected the tray of fruit and dates, and sized it up with a swift glance. She jiggled the tiny silver spoon in the cup to assure herself that it really did hold thick, solid threads of saffron. Only then did she continue on her way towards the middle room.

Welcome, Zarruuuuf, muttered Salima, with no attempt to keep the derision from her voice. My, my, you've come so early! If only you had waited awhile, say ten days or so. Now you'll have to excuse me, my leg is giving me trouble, it's painful enough that I can't get up to greet you.

Zarifa heaved her massive body to the floor at the foot of Mayya's bedding. She sucked in a slow breath. Relax, dearie, just keep yourself where you are resting, milady! Anyway, when did you ever get up for *Zarruuf*? She twisted the huge silver ring on her right index finger and leaned into the mat slightly. How are you doing, Mayya? Good girl, you're safe and sound, blessed with a good strong body and the baby, my girl... I'm so sorry, I couldn't come any earlier, because my boy Sanjar, just now he's got another baby girl.

Mabrukeen, Salima said. Double congratulations on your blessed addition! We didn't hear the news.

Zarifa leaned more heavily over the recumbent Mayya. Only yesterday. The viper Shanna had a girl, another daughter for Sanjar. We had our hands full.

Opposite Zarifa, Salima's response was to bend closer over her daughter. And today? she asked. Where've you been since dawn? You couldn't come to see your master's daughter? But of course, we have to remember the proverb-giver's words: The feet walk fast for the loving heart's sake, but when you feel no longing, your feet drag and ache.

Zarifa stretched herself out and narrowed her eyes. No, that's not the right proverb, habba! Listen, milady. You know perfectly well, the old bubber only eats Zarifa's bread. And the proverb-maker says: Who's fond of you, love him back, who shoves you away, shove him back, who keeps himself from you, give him the sack. Well! I see no one's been here to see you yet, no one whose coffee we'd be pouring out right now. Hand over the little girl, Mayya, I'll say some prayers for her, make some pleas up there.

The little girl wants to nurse, Salima interjected. Zarifa smiled and wiggled her shoulders lightly, like a dancer. Fish are good for her, you know, they'll make her milk come. Not so good when she's just given birth, Zarruuf, Salima snapped. Zarruf guffawed and sang out, The proverb-giver says: Give the sick what they yearn for, but it's God alone will restore. But why not some salted fish, since dear Abdallah already brought her forty hens? She must have her strength back! Even that viper of Sanjar's – he brought her a live chicken out of the goodness of his heart, and honey and butter too, and still she doesn't want me to cook for her. The proverb-spinner says: When the ass's belly is full of food, then and there he kicks you good. She's forgetting those days when she didn't even have a dishdasha to cover her body, way back before she married my boy. Ya ayni alayk, you poor boy, my Sanjar. Your luck took a wrong turn with that viper!

Get up, Mayya, sit up now and nurse the girl, muttered Salima, showing her disgust with her guest. Mayya struggled into a sitting position.

The viper who's with my boy nurses lying down, Zarifa sang out. Like a bitch dog. Won't even sit up. And she named the girl Rasha. My wretched son didn't say a word – well, what's he going to say? She'd bite the boy's flesh and poison him if he so much as said a word. Instead of naming them Habiba or Maryam or Fatima, they give them these names – Mervat, and Rabab, and Naabaab, Shaaakaaab, Daaaadaaaab, or maybe, why not, She-who-gouges-out-Satan's-eye? What a world it is! And you, Mayya, now what's your baby named?

Mayya was staring into the baby girl's face, nestled at her breast.

London.

There was a sudden silence. Zarifa dropped her head. Then she heaved her immense body off the floor. Must get myself moving, she muttered. Have to make lunch for you. She got to her feet heavily and headed for the kitchen.

Salima let her breath out slowly. She was worried that the

oily hue of the walls in here was darker and heavier than it ought to be for a new mother. Still, she preferred to keep her recovering daughter in this room because it was warm, and guests would see the shelves made by the little wall-openings stacked with fancy plates. The mandus, the old, elegantly worked wooden chest with its brass fittings that she'd had since her own wedding, added some grace to the room as well, especially since it had recently acquired a fresh gloss and a new layer of gilt paint on the fixings. And there were the cushions and the carpets embroidered and sewn with Indian silk. Salima was always very careful with décor and adornment, except when it came to her own body.

When the voice of the muezzin's wife sang out, asking permission to come in, Salima hurried over to the open end of the reception room to meet her. At the same moment Zarifa emerged from the kitchen, which sat at the eastern corner of the courtyard in front of the house. Well, just look there! Salima's legs are all better now, she can get up after all! she muttered loudly.

As Salima and the muezzin's wife were greeting each other with obvious warmth, Zarifa's loud hoarse voice sailed across the courtyard. The proverb-maker says: Morning or sunset, the beloved's loved ever, but no welcome for the other, though proud and clever! She slapped her palm across her thigh and disappeared back into the kitchen.

Years ago the muezzin's wife had come here from the town of Sama'il deep in the interior. Her own name was long forgotten since people had started calling her simply Muezzin-Wife. She and Salima launched themselves into a conversation that meandered and branched off into new tales, becoming ever more engrossing. Mayya stared at her nursing baby, her gaze silent and neutral.

Asma came in and sat down next to them. Listen, Mama! You have to make up this mixture for Mayya, just like the writer of this book *Fruit for the Wayfarer* said to do it. It's got—

With a laugh Salima interrupted her. I don't need any of your medicine books or those fancy dukhtoors teaching me what to make for my daughter. I brought up five living healthy souls, I did, and no one had to teach me how to do it. Those books will make your eyes pop out if you keep on reading them all the time. Come on, time for some coffee.

Look here, Mayya, said Asma. Modern medicine has established that dates are very good for a woman who has just given birth, and that was revealed in the Qur'an, too, after all, when Our Lady Maryam shook the palm tree and the dates fell down on her, and all around. She was in childbirth and in the Qur'an she was told, 'if you shake the palm-tree trunk, towards you, it will bring you fresh ripe dates.'

Asma pronounced the word *rutban* in the classical way with its proper grammatical ending, hoping to dazzle Muezzin-Wife. But her mother's firm hand around her arm yanked her away from her sister. Leave Mayya alone! She'll eat on her own, by herself, when she wants to.

Why? asked Asma. Muezzin-Wife had an answer ready and she intoned it half under her breath. Because she is unclean inside. It is not proper for people to share her food. It is not permitted to eat from the same platter as an unclean woman.

Asma was annoyed. She was certain there was a hadith on this. She was convinced that God's Messenger had said or shown somehow, in his own life, in what he told others, that a woman could eat and drink in company no matter what her condition. But in the presence of the muezzin's wife she could not say anything, since the woman might think she was criticizing the Faith.

Zarifa came in to pour their coffee. She had always been the only woman of slave origins who ate from the same platter of food as the free women did. In fact, she'd given herself this privilege, imposing it on the ladies. But no one had ever objected, or started an argument with her over it. Now she began tossing chunks of the sweet oily delicacy that marked special occasions into her mouth, licking the oil left on her fingers with obvious pleasure.

Take it easy on yourself, Zarifa, Muezzin-Wife muttered. Remember about your diabetes. Your body – ma sha' allah! – I wouldn't say it's exactly scrawny.

Zarifa cackled. What should scare me about being sugar-sick? Death comes when it comes, milady dear. No need for us to torture ourselves over it. And my body – ma sha' allah! – is just fine. May the envious one go blind! I don't listen to what those dukhtoors say. Sukkari, they say! Well, diabetes or no diabetes, I don't mind them. Anyway, as the proverb-maker says: The flesh of youth? Old age devours it! She refilled her cup and sipped, her bulging fingers slipping around the cup.

Muezzin-Wife smiled thinly. Seek God's forgiveness, Zarifa! The flesh of youth is devoured by old age? How much older, Zarifa? May God's forgiveness always be there, since humans have such tall hopes! You're at least fifty now.

Zarifa shrugged. So, what's fifty, ya habba! Fifty is the summit of youthfulness, I say. And my son's only just had a child. I didn't become a grandmother before I was even forty, like some folks do.

Salima acted as though she hadn't been paying attention and didn't understand the gist of the remark that Zarifa had flung her way. She busied herself eating orange sections. It did not bother her that she had become a grandmother while still in her early forties, and she made a little show of her indifference to Zarifa's comments. But Muezzin-Wife persisted. True, Zarifa, wAllahi, you aren't really elderly, but you were in too much of a hurry anyway. You married off your boy so young.

Zarifa sat up straighter, swallowed the sweet and looked the muezzin's wife straight in the eye. Mercy be! she said. I didn't realise Shanna was such a viper. Her father had just died, and one shows mercy to the dead. Her poor miserable mother, Masouda, went mad. The girl is a relative, I told myself. There's a connection from the womb, God forbid we abandon her. And I ask you, anyway, was it better to marry off Sanjar or to leave him to the mercy of all those men who know exactly what they're after?

Salima gave her a sharp look and Muezzin-Wife shook her head hard. Seek God's forgiveness for such talk, she exclaimed hastily.

More women's voices could be heard, asking leave to enter. Salima gave Asma a sign. She got to her feet sluggishly. Asma was not at all convinced that she had no right, as an unmarried girl, to sit with the married women and listen to their conversations, especially since the 'experience of life' that this custom of theirs tried so hard to keep from her was something she could obtain easily enough from books. Aah, the books! The thought of the enormous pleasure of books quickened Asma's pace. It was a good moment to lose herself in their joys.

Abdallah

As much as I have travelled, I still like getting the seat by the window. I like to stare down at one city after another, dwindling and then vanishing. Papa, London said once, you travel an awful lot. I did not say to her that when we are away from home, in new and strange places, we get to know ourselves better. And that is exactly the way it is with love. London does not know much about strange places or being far from home but she certainly knows about love. Her stubborn endurance under her mother's blows allured and pained me in equal measure, until I cracked the whip myself and married her to him.

What do you really know about love? she demanded of her mother. From the very first day you opened your eyes on life, you never saw anyone, until you saw my father. How old were you when they married you to him?

She thought I was out of the house at the time but I was there and I heard her say these things. Mayya laughed, but there was something almost violent in her laughter. Hearing it, I was frightened. And that was all – she didn't actually say anything. She did not say that she loved me, had ever loved me. She didn't say that at all.

Now my father is dying and I am suffocating.

The tubes going into his body sucked the life out of me. He mumbled things I couldn't make out, and it was I who cried, sitting there next to his bed until daylight came. Muhammad was only a year old and I was thinking of him, too, as I sat at the bedside of my dying father. London screamed when she found out he had died, and Mayya chided her. Your screams make the dead hurt, she told London. It had been a long time – it was years before – that she had said to me, Don't you see that you carry your respect for your father too far? I scolded her for saying such a thing.

Ustaz Mamduh said: I came as a service to patriotism and Arabism.

London said: I want a BMW, it suits my status as a doctor and as the daughter of the House of Merchant Sulayman. Why did London have to mention her ties of blood to her grandfather?

Salim said: I want the new PlayStation.

Zarifa said: Best we marry off this boy before something happens that we'll really regret.

My aunt said: Go to Muscat and don't worry, I'll see to things in the Big House.

My partner Abu Salih said: This deal is watertight.

Teacher Bill said: Why didn't you learn English when you were little? Now do you realise how important it is? It's the most important language in the world.

The most important language in the world. In the world. The world. The world is very big. Very small. My partner Abu Salih said, We're finished with the old ways of commerce. It's all about ads these days. That's what moves minds and opens pockets.

Pockets, pockets.

Papa, I said, I want a riyal. And he laughed. A whole riyal for a scruffy lad like you? In my days, we used to hope maybe one day we'd see a penny with our own eyes. One single little penny!

I wrote her name on the palm-tree trunk. I engraved it with hot metal onto the gate out at the farms. Mayya. The small world. The large world. No, thanks, I do not want any juice. I want shay. Yes, tea. More tea, please. Why is my head pounding? The stock exchange collapsed and Mayya screamed and moaned, You mean to say we aren't building the new house after all? she wailed. Our own three-storey house!

What was I to do? It collapsed. The stock collapsed. Mayya collapsed, Habib fled. Zarifa said he was raving. That's all, raving. Raving mad. He fled. My father went mad. He was on the cusp of old age. He threatened, he promised, and then he never returned to the subject. Zarifa returned to her old habits, freeing herself to take care of me.

On the day my father decided to marry her off to Habib, Zarifa tipped the paper horn of pepper into my mouth and poured it all down. Then she grabbed my ear, squeezed it hard, and said, If you tell anyone I did this, your father will truss you up and hang you upside down from the palm tree.

I didn't have anyone to tell, anyway. The pepper burnt my throat all the way down. I drank lots and lots of water, and when night came I could not find Zarifa. I could not find Zarifa's embrace to hide myself in.

My partner Abu Salih said: We'll take on this deal. My cousin said: Buy a building. Real estate is the safest thing in this country. This country. Everything in this country changes with astonishing speed.

London said: I don't like this al-Khuwayr neighbourhood. Papa, there's nowhere to walk.

Don't exaggerate, London.

Papa, all these streets are designed for cars' feet, not people's feet.

Then she forgot all about it, once she and her friends started to get absorbed in their never-ending expeditions from one mall to the next, in her car.

I love the capital! said Salim. True, it isn't Dubai, but we can find everything we want here. I didn't ask him what exactly it was that he wanted.

Muhammad didn't say much at all. Not then, and not ever in his life. Neither he nor Salim made me as happy as London did. When she was born the world couldn't contain me for happiness. She was pretty and cute and she looked a lot like Mayya. At the time, Zarifa swore that she would not enter Salima's house. She would not go in there and do her duty, pouring the coffee for all the women who would come to visit. I said to her, But this new baby is my daughter, mine, and Mayya is my wife. Why are you thinking of Salima? What does she have to do with this? She said she could not stand to see Salima, and she would not darken the door into Salima's home.

When Mayya had Muhammad, she said, I will not go to my family's house to rest up. I'm staying here. I'll have a maid to help.

In the graduation ceremony I was given my secondary diploma. I held onto it tightly. That evening, I showed it to my father. I was breathing hard. He laughed. Why are you panting like a dog in front of everyone? You won't gain anything from that bit of paper. *This* is what will help you, he said, and he patted the pocket of his dishdasha. He laughed.

He laughed. Laughed!

I couldn't find anyone to ask. No one would tell me how she died. When I got older I asked my aunt. It was the basil bush that killed her, she said.

At conferences, every so often they place flowers along the tables. But never basil …

How could this be, Auntie? How could a basil bush kill someone?

She waved my question away.

Zarifa despised my aunt. When my father died and I

moved to Muscat she went to join her son Sanjar in Kuwait. How could my mother die because of a basil plant, Zarifa?

I don't know.

But – you know everything, Zarifa.

Hooting, she yanked me close. Clutched to her chest I could smell her sweat, mingled as ever with that chicken-broth scent. I am Zarruuf, she said. That's all I am. And I never know everything. I know how to cook, I know how to eat, how to dance, and I know— She made the kind of obscene gesture I'd begun to notice a lot, from men, from women, as soon as the fuzz began to show across my upper lip.

Yes, I did steal my father's rifle. I went with Zarifa's son Sanjar and our friend Marhun to hunt magpies. Sanjar warned me, If you don't get hold of that rifle you're not a man. Marhun added, And if you don't come, we'll roast you instead of the magpies. Anyway, once we were in the desert they attacked me and held me down. They tried to force me to say it: I am the slave, I am Abdallah the slave of Sanjar and Marhun.

But I didn't say that. Instead, I said, I'll tell Zarifa everything. So they left me alone. But they ate the magpies all by themselves. I swore that when I grew up I would eat a hundred magpies all by myself. But by the time I was nearly grown up it was against the law to hunt magpies.

Mayya never planted any basil. She liked growing native wild roses, sweet-smelling jasmine and also the other kind of jasmine that has a strong and piercing smell, as well as daisies and greens, lemon trees and quince bushes. The courtyard was vast, and she commandeered most of it for gardening. Once I asked her, Why aren't you sewing, Mayya? You silly man, she said, you don't understand anything. Why should I go on sewing when there are seamstresses everywhere you turn? And to be honest, I'm tired of it. But she got tired of studying, too, in just the same way. She lost hope about learning English and stopped going to evening classes. When I suggested we enrol Muhammad in the Hope School for special-needs children, she cried and cried. Then she said, My son is just like all the other boys. He'll go to school just like his brother and his cousins. Muhammad was not like all the other children, but she did not want to see that. She never planted any basil. One night – it was a clear, quiet night – I asked her what she would think about maybe planting some basil? Its smell brings vipers! she said. On the night after the magpie hunt, Zarifa dressed my wounds – which were pretty bad – with salt and turmeric. All the while I babbled, asking one single question over and over. How did she die, Zarifa? How did my mama die?

Zarifa had not said a word all night. But now, finally, she said, Abdallah, my boy! You know what the proverb-maker says. Ignorance is bliss.

When Khawla began driving her car, Mayya suddenly insisted on learning how to drive. But she failed the test. The police were prejudiced against her, she announced. They were in conspiracy with Khawla. Mayya was sure of that. Khawla was pretty and she had style; there was an elegance about the way she did things. I hired a driver for Mayya but she threw him out after a few months. Mayya! I said. What have you done now! But all she could say was, Ya rajul, ya rajul, chiding me as though, being a man, I just didn't understand. After Khawla's divorce, when she opened a beauty salon in one of Muscat's fanciest neighbourhoods, Mayya tried again to get a licence.

I did not listen to my cousin. I did not buy a building. I bought shares and then the stock market crashed. There was a lot of funny business that went on but the newspapers were quiet about it. They didn't even print anything about the rape of Hanan and her schoolmates in the south.

Hanan was teaching at an elementary school way in the

south, in Salalah Town, near the border It was the middle of the night when London phoned us. A gang of teenaged boys had assaulted the teachers' dormitory, she said. There had been rapes. Hanan – she was raped. And people were silent. Who bought this loud silence? London nearly went mad. She stayed in the hospital with Hanan, her good friend, who had had a nervous breakdown.

I stayed next to my father in the hospital. Over and over, I moistened his dry lips with drops of water, and closed his eyes. And then I cried. Though I didn't shed a single tear in front of people after his funeral. In my pressed white dishdasha, wearing my dagger and the requisite coloured turban, I remained there, at home, from morning to sundown, the entire three days, shaking hands with all of the men who came to offer condolences. Over and over I murmured, Al-baqaa lillah. Our lives are in God's hands, their lives go on in ours. The well-wishers ate meat and rice and went away. In the evenings, I closed myself into his room. Something burned inside me, though I didn't, and don't, know what it was. Something was consuming me. In the hospital, my father in a coma, I pushed the turban back from the top of my forehead and brought the scars of my deep wound, still so visible, as close as I could to his open eyes. Then I pushed the robe off my shoulder which still carried the harsh marks of knife blades and rough palm-fibre ropes.

Do you remember the day of the magpies? I whispered to him. He did not move. The hand that had tied me up in palm fibres and had thrust me down the well to dangle there head-first for what seemed like hours, my head and body colliding against the edges of its stone walls, did not move. I whispered again, into his ear. Sanjar is a little younger than me, yes, like you said. But Sanjar dared me to steal the rifle. I was going to put it back where it belonged. I would have put it back, but Marhun told on me.

He didn't move. I raised my voice. Sanjar fled, you didn't hit Marhun, and I nearly died of fear, hanging upside down in the total blackness of the well, tied up in palm fibres and no idea when I might be untied.

The hand that had done all of that no longer moved. The hand remained there, passive, fused to the feeding tubes, completely motionless. I seized it. I moved it along the bumpy traces of my wounds. I pressed it hard into my flesh and burst into hopeless, desperate tears.

Asma

Asma went into the big room that the girls shared. Remote from the rest of the house, it was like a growth that had attached itself to the far corner of the courtyard. When Mayya and her sisters had reached a certain age, their mother began to worry. She would feel easier if they could be kept apart from the main bulk of the house. She didn't want them to run into male relatives who might come into the main reception room. After all, men from the clan could appear at any time, coming to fulfil some family obligation. She asked her husband to have this room in the courtyard built for them.

As usual, Khawla was scrunched over in front of her mirror, but she had a small and unfamiliar object in her hands. What's that, Khawla? Asma squatted down next to her sister. Khawla whispered the answer. Lipstick!

Asma gasped, took it from her sister's hand, and inspected it. Bright red inside, the lipstick was concealed by its awesome shell, in the shape of a golden bird. Where did you get this thing? Asma asked her sister.

Khawla snatched it away from her. I asked Mayya to buy it for me in Muscat before she went in to the hospital to have the baby. Asma stared at the fancy golden bird and muttered, But my mother . . .

Khawla looked her in the eye. My mother won't know anything about it unless… Asma nodded to reassure her and moved away, turning to the shelf where the books were now lined up, after their rescue from the damp and rot in the storeroom. She pawed through them until she found the volume bound in blue and read the title out in a loud voice. *Musnad al-Imam al-Rabi' bin Habib. The Well-Supported Prophetic Traditions Compiled by the Imam al-Rabi' bin Habib*. Turning over the dog-eared, disintegrating title page, she read the uneven scrawl on the page beneath:

> The owner of this book, who beseeches for God's mercy, is Masoud bin Hamid bin Muhammad, it having come into my possession as a gift from my friend and brother, Ali bin Salim bin Muhammad. I inscribe these words on this page, with my own hand, fleetingly mortal though it may be.

Asma did not like handwriting. It always reminded her of the day the school had opened in al-Awafi, a few years back. The school had opened but girls older than ten weren't allowed in. They would only be admitted to the basic adult literacy classes, and those didn't even begin to happen until some time later. Asma had heard that some of the lads who showed themselves able to write out their first names were allowed right away into the third grade, whatever their real age was. She hadn't known how that could happen, since she was not there on the first day anyway. She was already too old to try for it. Then she was entered on the books for the adult literacy classes even though she wasn't actually old enough for those. She had barely reached middle school when they closed down the classes. They said there weren't enough students. In her sloppy, sloping hand, the teacher wrote on the blackboard: Classes are cancelled due to lack of numbers. Asma walked out of the school. Ever since, uneven handwriting had made her sick.

Instead of preserving the beauty of your eyes you blind them through reading, Khawla remarked. Asma responded, but half under her breath. Shut up, stupid! Ever since you left school two years ago you haven't so much as cracked a book's cover open. Hardly even the Holy Book! If it weren't for my mother's whip hand in Ramadan you would never open it at all.

Khawla shrugged scornfully and turned her back, gazing again into her mirror. Asma skipped through some pages and suddenly, catching a particular passage, she smiled. She read it out loud.

> Abu Hurayra, may God be pleased with him, recited: When the Messenger of God (may God's prayers and mercy be upon him) was praying, he said to his wife, Aisha, hand me my robe. She said, But I am having my period. He said, That isn't your fault and it doesn't matter.

I was sure there was something, Asma bayed. I knew it! But Muezzin-Wife . . .

Asma began repeating the Prophet's words to herself until she had memorised the passage. She wanted to tell her mother and Mayya every word. She giggled, imagining what a tizzy this would send Muezzin-Wife into – seeing them all eating together, in the knowledge that childbirths and periods and what have you didn't soil anyone. She returned the book to its place amongst the others – *Fruit for the Wayfarer* with its ordinary paperbound cover, the *Mustatraf* bound in red velvet and printed at the Mahmudiyya Press in Cairo, the collection of poetry by the famous ancient Arab poet Antara in its leather binding and inside the old-fashioned lithograph type and the close handwritten commentary in the margins. There was also the book called *The Stories of the Prophets*, a small and worn volume printed in Calcutta, as well as a large tome, the pages yellowed, which was, the title page announced, Part Two of *The Unique Necklace* by the noble Imam Shihab al-Din Ahmad, Alone of his Age, the Era's Sage, known (as it also said) as Ibn 'Abd Rabbih, Son of the Servant of his Lord, from Andalusia, of the Malekite School of Islamic Law, God shower His beneficence on him and let him dwell in God's broadest green paradise, Amen. In the margin (the title page went on to say) is inscribed the text *Zahr al-adab wa-thamar al-albab* by Abu Ishaq Ibrahim bin Ali, he who was known as al-Husari of Qayrawan, of the Malekite legal School of Islam, may God Almighty bless him.

Sometimes Asma's father asked her to read to him from this tome. She found it difficult to follow the cramped script. Just as trying, Asma would find herself suddenly having to awkwardly shorten certain expressions containing words she was embarrassed to read out loud in her father's presence.

On her shelf also was the story of Tawaddud the Jariya, a small book with a few pages ripped out. Years later Asma would remember two things about this story: the absence created by the ripped pages, and the simile comparing Tawuddud the Slave-Girl's neck to the graceful stem of a silver ewer.

There was also the blue-spined book called *Kalila and Dimna*, the fables said to have been authored originally in Sanskrit by the Indian philosopher Bidpai, translated into Persian, and then translated into Arabic by the scholar Abdallah Ibn al-Muqaffa – a diminutive book no taller than a hand span, looking more like a little school notebook – printed at Sadir Press in Beirut in 1927. There was one passage from *Kalila* that Asma particularly liked to read out loud to Khawla, for its lyrical beauty, created by the repeated *aa*s and *haa*s, the feminine possessive pronoun at the end of so many nouns. *Qaala al-ghuraab: za'amuu anna ardan min aradi* ... The crow said: They claimed that after the passage of years, lands where the elephants dwelt went dry. The water grew scarce, the wells dried up, the vegetation was killed off, the trees withered away and the elephants grew very thirsty ...

There were also some books furnished by the Ministry of Heritage. Asma had begun reading some sections headed 'On Matters of Purity' but they were too boring and she stopped. They were odd, too – the very specific instructions that she couldn't figure out, because they appeared to make no sense. For example, that one must do one's intimate business on a soft surface rather than a hard one so that one's pee sinks in rather than ricocheting and possibly soiling one's body. Yet every bathroom she'd ever seen had hard surfaces. Another point she had fretted over was the legists' directive on always wiping yourself with stones before you cleaned yourself with water. Never mind that people didn't always live in the desert now! There were many other such instructions, which were apparently changeless since they were never updated in these texts, even though some of these books of the jurisprudents' rules that Asma tried to read had been published quite recently. Asma only glanced at the thin little English-language books Mayya had bought from The Family Bookstore in Muscat before her marriage. No one could read them but Mayya had doggedly persisted in picking them up and even leafing through them.

As she always did, before turning away from the bookshelf Asma riffled through the few pages remaining from a book whose title she did not know. She had kept it apart from the other fragile, deteriorating books in the storeroom. In these pages she read that text, though she already knew it by heart, even if she did not understand it at all.

Some of those who fancy themselves philosophers claim that God, Mighty is He, created every soul in the shape of a ball. And then He split every one of these spheres into two, and apportioned to each and every human body one half. It is decreed that each body will meet the body that holds the other half of that rent soul. Between the two a passion arises from that ancient bond. From one human being to the next, the effect of this union will vary, according to the delicacy of each person's nature.

Qamar, the Moon

Salima's husband was returning from the evening's conviviality at the nomads' settlement when he was overpowered by a mad ecstasy. The sand under Azzan's feet was very soft; he had slipped off his sandals to enjoy the quiet coolness of the desert surface. The full moon kept him friendly company, sending familiar shadows across the sandy mounds. From afar appeared the lights of al-Awafi, muted and remote, as though the village were a faraway world he did not know. He'd spent half the night in storytelling and conversation with his Bedouin friends – the usual singing and laughter, the music of a flute and a rebec.

Azzan had decided to return to al-Awafi on foot, turning down the offer of a ride in any of his friends' four-wheel-drive jeeps. The homes of the Bedouin scattered beneath the lip of the vast sand dune were not very far away from al-Awafi, but at no point did the two settlements overlap. Al-Awafi held fast to the immobile stability of its agricultural roots. The Bedouin – despite all appearances of permanence, having settled in one locale and replaced their camelhair tents with cement block dwellings – scorned, even despised, the very idea of putting down roots. They relied first and foremost on pasturing camels and sheep. They held fast to their traditional loose garments and their free, untethered natures, preserving the impermeable boundaries that separated them from what was called 'the life of the settled'.

These evening sessions were the only thing that could lift Azzan out of his gloom and depression. Mingling with his Bedouin friends, he could keep that heavy cloud from settling over his heart, from convincing him that stories and laughter were nothing but the banal and trivial games of this fleeting lower world, this den of sorrows. When he was with them, amidst the singing, the memory of his two dead sons no longer caught in his throat like a lump and he didn't feel so weighed down by the world that all he wanted was to vanish and leave its false pretences behind. When he was with them, the notion that one could feel some joy at the pleasures of this world no longer churned up pangs of guilt from deep inside him. He could enjoy himself without the lurking worry that it was all a chimera he must avoid; he needed to be as alert to its dangers as he was on guard against the most vicious of traps.

As he walked over the sands, he repeated in his head some of the verses they'd sung, trying to match his steps to the beat of the tune. The face of his newborn granddaughter appeared to him. He was only in his mid-forties but he had become a grandfather! Suddenly eager, he felt an urge to reach home *right now*, to go into the middle room where he would see her tiny face, asleep. He smiled to himself and was on the point of humming a tune when he was startled by the sight of a human shadow between the rises of sand. In the name of God! he muttered, and took two quick steps back. But the shadow came towards him slowly and without any flicker of hesitation.

Who's there? Azzan called out.

Me.

He was startled to hear a woman's voice coming back to

him. A moment's silence, and a tall woman stood close before him. She pulled off her burqu. He felt himself somehow grow calmer.

Who are you and what do you want?

The woman met his gaze with utter directness. Her pure, resolute beauty and the steady gleam in her large eyes disconcerted him. Her piercingly sweet fragrance and the way she stood right there – so close to him! – was even more disturbing. But it was her words that truly made him lose what was his already fragile sense of control.

I am Najiya. I am Qamar, the Moon. It is you I want.

For many years to come these words would reverberate through his head. *I am Najiya, I am the Moon, Qamar, and it is you I want*. Azzan had not known many women in the course of his life. Certainly he had never known a woman of such resolution and valour, a woman called after the moon itself. She deserved an even greater name than that, he would muse. She was more beautiful than any image he had ever seen or would ever see again in the whole of his life. In the moonlight she looked like he imagined an houri of Paradise must look, those women of heaven above, of whom God had given tidings to His believing servants. Now she swayed toward him, a silent movement that spoke her resolve. He gripped his sandals, shoved them tightly under his arm and fled, running as fast as he could in the direction of al-Awafi, unable to think a single thought about anything at all.

Najiya did not return home. She went to her friend's. Standing outside the wood door she shouted. Khazina! Khaziiiiinaaa!

Still arranging the burqu over her face, her friend came out. All well, Qamar?

Come on, said Najiya. Come and stay at my place tonight.

They walked for a long time before Najiya's home came

into view. My brother is camped out on the eastern sand bank, so we can sleep inside.

Khazina didn't say anything until they had sat down, face to face.

What happened?

He ran away, her friend answered quietly.

Khazina laughed so hard she crumpled flat onto the floor. God forbid! He's no man! He ran away? Hahaha! He ran away from you, Qamar?

Najiya did not laugh. She waited until her friend stopped shrieking.

I want him. I will have him.

Khazina wiped the tears from her eyes with the edge of her robe and tossed a piece of wood onto the fire. Qamar, this man doesn't seem much use.

Najiya stretched herself. But I want him. And he will come to me. When the Moon longs for something, the Moon gets her desire.

Khazina shook her head. Sister, this man is married to the daughter of Shaykh Masoud, and he's the shaykh of their whole clan. You think he will leave her to marry you?

Najiya laughed that famous, ringing laugh of hers that revealed her pearl-like teeth. She really does deserve that nickname, Khazina said to herself. She's the Moon in full. No wonder people have all but forgotten her real name.

Slowly and elaborately Najiya extended her arms over and behind her head. Who said I want to marry him? Qamar doesn't let anyone give her orders. I wasn't created to serve and obey some man. Some fellow who would steal what should be mine and keep me from seeing my brother and my girlfriends! One day saying, No, you cannot go out, another time saying, No, don't even get dressed, don't even think about going out! One minute saying, Come here! and the next, Go away! No, no, Khazina – Azzan will be mine but I won't be his. He'll come to me when I want him, and he'll go away when I say so. Ever since I saw him that evening, sitting with the others, talking and laughing, I knew this man would be Qamar's. And he runs away? He flees? That man scampered off, like I was a jinni taking him by surprise, so he fled! Refuse me? Qamar? There's never yet been a man created who can refuse me, Khazina. Azzan will come to me on his knees.

In silence the friends watched the fire die down until they were drowsy enough to fall asleep.

Najiya lived in two rooms opening onto a reception room that overlooked the courtyard, with a low wall that went only halfway up to the roofing. But when she was growing up, home had been a tent. Her father couldn't hang onto money. She had never seen her mother and she never bothered asking about her. She had one love in this world – her little brother. The scars on her body were the traces of old wounds picked up in the fights she'd had defending him from other boys. She would hurry home every day from primary school to ask him who had hurt him today. Stuffing her yellow school pinafore inside her loose trousers she would go and confront them, in another day of fights. By the time the lads stopped beating her brother or calling him Mental, she was already in middle school. That was when she began figuring out that she hadn't been created to sit in a hot, humid classroom with fifty other girls listening to strange words about grammar and numbers and science from dawn until the late-afternoon call to prayer. She thoroughly disliked the white school shoes they had to wear, with the plasticky soles that turned blackish after no more than a week, and the utterly plain grey middle-school uniform which was always crumpled and damp from the hot, crowded space. The strange dialects spoken by the Egyptian and Sudanese women who taught them made her uncomfortable, and she never got used to the idea of sitting in one little place all day long. Leaving school saved her from having to ride stuffed into a pickup truck with ten other Bedouin girls, their small bodies vibrating, buffeted by the wind and stung by the sand particles it slapped across them, for an hour or more before they reached the school building.

Her father was oblivious to anything but his raucous sessions – men grilling meat and drinking, and the zar exorcisms – and so Najiya took over. She handled all his property. She tended his sheep and camels, and in a few years their numbers doubled. She fed their thoroughbred she-camels dates, country samna and honey, and entered them in the races until she succeeded in selling one to a shaykh from Abu Dhabi for twenty thousand riyals. She had to get a passport for the camel, whom she had named Gazelle, before shipping her off to Abu Dhabi. When the money came, she replaced the tent with a reinforced concrete house. She bought carpets and fancy wooden trousseau-chests from the Matrah souq. She openly mocked her neighbours, who had built a full two-storey house but still did their business under the desert rush-bushes right outside, even though their new house had five bathrooms.

Najiya did not give in to her brother's condition, either. She would not let him stay idle. She trained him to tend the camels and sheep. Her father's death came as a relief. Now she could truly consolidate her authority over her life, her property and her freedom. As her developing womanhood started to draw attention, and word of her beauty spread near and far, people began calling her Qamar for she was as radiant as the moon. Making light of the suitors who flocked to the house, she devoted herself completely to her brother and to her growing wealth. When she saw the right man, she told herself, she would know him – and she would take him. She selected her friends carefully. She sold her distinctive Bedouin needlework, and her home became a magnet for visitors and a refuge for those in need. Woman or man, Najiya's acquaintances held her in respect and a lot of awe.

When her brother suddenly developed polio and couldn't move, she closed up her house. For months she lived with him in the faraway hospitals of the government, relying on the women she had befriended to take care of her flock. Time after time, the hospital authorities expelled her from the men's section where her brother was kept. Najiya simply rolled herself up in her blanket and slept in a corridor. The doctors told her openly, as well as by insinuation, that her brother was a congenital 'Mongoloid'. Now his legs would never work again, and so what hopes did she still have for him? When people urged her to look forward to his salvation through death she turned her back on them. When she lost hope in the hospitals she carried him home and shut the two of them in, closing the doors to others. She treated him herself, for a long time, trying everything that experienced healers prescribed and then treatments she devised anew, concocting various herbal mixtures. She rubbed his legs with hot olive oil and crushed cloves. She tried to get him to stand up by leaning on her. She took his weight on her strong back and dragged his legs around the room, back and forth, trying to get him to walk. She blended colocynth with makhyasa herbs and made him drink the bitter stuff every morning, wiping away his saliva with her sleeve. She would never allow that look of futility in his slit-like eyes to deflect her or to defuse her determination. She shut her ears to anyone who mocked her attempts and she vowed her life to her brother.

When Najiya bint Said opened the door to her house and slaughtered a pair of camels for almsgiving, her brother was walking on his own two feet.

Abdallah

You keep up this aura of friendly care but what are you really thinking and feeling, my hostess of the air, as you spend all your waking days suspended between sky and earth? I was just like you, hanging between the heavens and the earth, when I saw her first.

I saw her on the day after the Greater Bairam Feast, in the month of Pilgrimage. My father went to pay his respects to her mother, Salima, as was the custom during the important ritual periods, for she was a distant relative of ours. I wasn't with him but I understood later that he particularly noticed Khawla, the youngest daughter. The next morning he said to me, I want you to go to Azzan's house for me. I was over there yesterday to give the family our feast day greetings and I left my walking stick there.

Somehow I knew that my father would not forget his walking stick anywhere. That rod was moulded to his hand on the very day he was created. What's more, I thought, he would not send me off to retrieve it when he could ask one of his retainers to go and get it. As usual though, I didn't raise these questions with him. I went to Azzan's home, and at the door I called out, asking permission to go in, letting them know I was there. I walked across the wide courtyard and entered the big room. But it seems Mayya hadn't realised I was coming in, she hadn't heard anything or noticed my entrance, and so she hadn't budged. She was sitting at the far end of the room on a wooden chair, trying to thread the needle on a sewing machine. It was a black Farrasha and she was bent over it, a pale, delicate, mysteriously remote figure. I caught a glimpse of her face and the ache there touched the agony inside me. Her short nose and her cheekbones, indeed her entire face, rose and fell with her intense concentration as she tried to poke the thread through the needle eye. She was leaning so far over the machine that it all but supported her entire body. Hunched over it, her paleness shone out in the daylight and the expression of pain across her small face was unbearable.

Looking hard at me – or perhaps scrutinizing my wandering gaze – her mother said to me, When I find the walking stick I will send it over. I tried hard to concentrate my thoughts on what phrases should be uttered in these circumstances but I couldn't find the appropriate words.

Salima looked to me like a woman who took charge of matters. She was still known around here as the Bride of the Falaj. Her skin was very light and her figure tended to fullness, accentuated by a round face, clear, smooth skin, an aquiline nose and piercing eyes. It was immediately obvious that Mayya did not take after her at all. I cast a last glance along the long room. I could not believe how much pain was crackling through the air, generated simply by Mayya's being there. Haloes of light embraced that presence. If I were to just put my hand out, I felt, I could touch those matchless haloes ever so gently. But Salima, ever her mother, suggested strongly, if indirectly, that it was time for me to go home. So I slunk out.

I left the house of Azzan not really understanding what had just taken place or what might be expected to happen next or in the future. A few years before this I had begun to field allusions to my 'flight' from girls. I wasn't fleeing, that wasn't it at all. But I felt no sense of participation, of presence, in any of it. The racy jokes the maids told and the way their hands wandered now and then onto my body didn't make me feel particularly loved, and I certainly didn't feel any desire or fondness towards them. Shanna chased me behind the lemon trees in the farm when I was barely fourteen and fell on me without any advance warning. Feeling dizzy and slightly sick, I pushed her away, spattering her with mud as I did so. She swore up and down that I would pay the price for it. Only a few days later, Zarifa was trying to push me into having sex with one or another daughter of the slave families that had long inhabited my father's household. These forays were sudden and rude, and completely without emotion. Most of these girls were either too afraid to say no, or they were bent on acquiring some gifts. The whole thing just made me turn more strongly inward. It drove Zarifa mad. She had come to see me and the state she thought I was in as an easy target for men's wayward desires, not to mention those of boys older than me. She was trying to protect me with whatever wiles she had up her sleeve, but her tricks wounded my young adolescence.

When I saw Mayya, I was beyond all of that. I was nineteen years old. Even so, I didn't understand what had just hit me on that night.

Zarifa did understand. I remember a particular day, at dawn. I remember the feeling of fullness I had – such happiness and pain together! Mayya's pale face distracted me utterly, took me far away from my mundane days, and filled me like nothing else had in my short experience of life. For the first time ever, that morning, I found myself pacing through our spacious home with its large rooms that had accumulated over time, one built up against another, and each one opening out onto the next. Yet I felt like the place wasn't big enough for me. I felt I was carrying something that was both heavy and precious, but at the same time I thought might just be able to take off and fly, because I felt so utterly light in my skin.

The night before – once I made certain that my father was asleep – I had snuck out to the eastern courtyard to sit under the enormous acacia tree where I could give myself up to the beautiful wailing of Suwayd's oud and his welcome company. The more I asked Suwayd, How did you do it, how did you get this oud? the harder he laughed. Hey, the same way one gets one's children, Shaykh – it's all a blessing and a gift from Allah!

For my part, Suwayd's words seemed to express perfectly my acquisition of the light that broke up the darkness of my days, that gentle fierce light. Was this what people called love? A gift, like the blessed livelihoods God grants to us. Now, I walked out of our house, away from its ornately decorated reception rooms, and I breathed in the blue dawn. I paced the length of the eastern courtyard, bordered by a row of lemon and mango trees punctuated by a single wild native rose bush. I felt such a yearning to sing in exactly the way Suwayd had sung the night before but I couldn't regulate the quavering rhythms of my voice, so instead I floated in the fragrances of lemon and rose. Somewhere out here had grown the basil bush that my mother had uprooted, and so it had killed her; still, even now, I could almost smell its fragrance. Would my mother have liked Mayya? Might she even have been fond of her? Or would she have exclaimed, as my father would on a later occasion, Oh, but I thought her name was Khawla!

No, Father, I said to him. Khawla is her younger sister. Mayya is the older one.

The older one? he muttered. You mean that skinny dark one? Didn't you see Khawla? Boy, what's happened to your eyesight, can't you tell the pretty sister from the others? Anyway, this Mayya you talk about is older than you. I remember Azzan, her father, parading her around on the feast day once, and the little girl was already walking. And that's when your mother was pregnant with you.

My voice was hoarse as I tried to answer. Only a year and eight months, Papa! He waved his cane around, the cane he had never once left behind at Azzan's house.

A few days later I wrote a letter to my father. I opened it in the customary way: In the name of God ... followed by the usual stuff: To my dear, esteemed and honourable father ... and I rounded it off with my signature: Your servant and son who humbly awaits your kindness, Abdallah. By now I have forgotten exactly what that letter said. My aunt – his sister – may have interceded on my behalf, too, and I know for certain that Zarifa confronted him with my inhibitions and my shamefaced attitude to girls which in her view were completely unwarranted. A few days later, he summoned me into his presence. He told me that he would betroth Mayya to me and would pay her a dowry of two thousand riyals. He would build a new set of rooms onto the eastern courtyard, with a modern bathroom. I would live in this annexe with my bride.

That dawn I walked barefoot across the pebbles, unaware then that most of this courtyard would disappear, swallowed up by the promised marital abode. I followed the line of the trees and turned into the narrow passageway to the western courtyard which was carpeted in sand rather than soft pebbles and seemed smaller than its eastern counterpart. In all of al-Awafi ours was the only house I had ever seen that had two open courtyards surrounding it, on two of its four sides. Was that why the townspeople had named it the Big House? I wondered.

The Big House is the place I inhabit with my father, where

sometimes we are visited by my aunt – his sister – and with us, in one of its many added-on rooms, live Zarifa and Sanjar, and Habib before he fled. Outside the house, but not far away from it, in very small huts live Suwayd and his brother Zaatar, and Zayd – before he drowned in the flash flood – with his wife Masouda and their daughter Shanna, plus Hafiza and her mother Saada and her three daughters whose paternal lineage is not known. All of them slaves, or at least somehow my father's inherited property.

The Big House, spacious as it was, hardly seemed to have any empty spaces. Guests of various ages and origins were always arriving and often they stayed on. A bundled cord of wood to the side of the western courtyard and those huge black cooking pots sitting out ready for use, were a familiar sight. Zarifa and Hafiza rarely cooked in the house's small inside kitchen, for the constant meals that had to be prepared for large numbers demanded the use of cauldrons too big for that narrow indoor cooking space. Similarly, the ritual slaughter, which was generally undertaken by Suwayd and Zaatar, took place here: the carcasses were hung and skinned in the western courtyard so they could be cooked immediately over an already-lit fire in the guest-kitchen where Zarifa baked bread too. Zarifa swore there was no comparison between meat roasted over 'real fire' and meat stewed in pots, which she called 'gas-fire meat'.

On that dawn I was packed tightly with thoughts, hopes and worries, and at the same time I felt buoyant and festive. Even the soot from the cooking fire that blackened the walls of the outside kitchen – just three walls and roofing held up by wood stakes – I didn't find ugly. Everything was beautiful: the sand, the pots, the aroma of the baking flat bread rising from inside the kitchen and floating toward the courtyard. I went in to the bare shelter of the open kitchen, doorless to allow more room for the huge pots. I found Zarifa in there, perched on two Nido powdered milk cans, her body spilling over them as she bent over the hot baking brick, pounding out the dough, stretching it across the surface and seconds later dragging it back up off the brick with wondrous skill. She didn't even turn around as she said, Good morning, Abdallah, my boy. Or should I say, Ya hababi, Milord, since it seems you've become quite the big man now!

Zarifa knew, then. I didn't say anything. Had she seen Mayya's name scratched onto the tree trunks and scrawled across the pages in my notebooks? But Zarifa couldn't read!

How did you know, Zarifa?

She cackled, the sound loud in that quiet early morning. Sonny, as the proverb-maker says: A human hand spread wide can't block the sun outside.

So I got married, you see, my kind and pleasant air hostess, whose artificial smile makes me feel such pity for you. I dislike fake smiles as strongly as I do laughter. Mayya – that's my wife, my dear hostess – did not laugh on her wedding day. She didn't even smile.

Motherhood

Just before dawn, Mayya was sitting up on her bedding, the nursing baby in her lap. Her newborn daughter had finally stopped wailing and dropped off to sleep. Mayya tipped her tired aching head back against the wall. She sensed, more than she saw, the dark, shiny oily blue-green colour on the walls, giving off a hard light that hurt her eyes. Closing them, she could see the maternity wing at the Saada Hospital, the salt and oil placed on the newborn's belly button, the wife of Abdallah's uncle in Wadi Aday. The women visiting every morning, afternoon, and evening, fresh chicken broth, Zarifa's saliva as she blew into the face of the baby girl and repeated half-intelligible supplications to the Divine for her protection, that enormous silver ring Zarifa wore, the white swaddling, the newborn's tiny red tongue and her fingernails which were not allowed to be clipped lest she become a thief in her future life.

Mayya opened her eyes and studied her daughter. Her body was scrawnier than the bodies of most newborns and her scream was particularly sharp. Mayya passed her hand over the baby's thin layer of black hair. She could not suppress the incredulity she felt. So this is motherhood then?

Every day, Asma would ask her, So what does it feel like,

motherhood? Is it the greatest feeling in the world? Mayya wouldn't answer. All she felt was exhaustion, pains in her back and belly, and an urgent need to bathe. Her itchy scalp, which made her want to constantly rub her fingers into her hair, was simply no longer bearable. Finally her mother permitted her to have a quick bath but only on condition that the water didn't touch her hair. After all, colds stalked brand-new mothers, Salima would remind her. And if their hunt was successful, well, we all know that fever is fatal to new mothers... Meanwhile, tiresome Asma went on asking about motherhood and what she called the warm intimacy of nursing! But all that nursing meant, as far as Mayya could see, was no sleep all night long and a constant struggle with the baby to get her to open her mouth, not to mention the back pain she had after sitting in the same position for so many hours. Mayya didn't say any of this to Asma, though. Listening to her sister kept her occupied, and she didn't have to say anything as long as Asma was chattering on.

Mayya considered silence to be the greatest of human acts, the sum of perfection. When you were utterly quiet and still you were likeliest to hear accurately what others were saying. And whenever Mayya felt bored with their words she listened to herself in the bubble of silence she had created around her. If she said nothing, then nothing could cause her pain. Most of the time, she had nothing to say. And there were moments when she might have something to say but knew she didn't want to speak. The muezzin's wife approved and even pronounced a blessing over Mayya's silence. On the Day of Judgement it will be known that your tongue has created no complaint against you.

Once this child of hers was much older, after Salim and Muhammad had arrived in the world as well, Mayya made another discovery: sleep. Sleep! She would sleep and sleep, and as long as she stayed asleep nothing could harm her. She came to realise that sleep was an even greater miracle than silence, since when she slept she did not even have to hear what others were saying. Asleep, she would not be speaking, nor would others speak to her. In her sleep she saw nothing, not even dreams. Entering the realm of sleep meant coming into a place of no responsibilities where she felt nothing, and the things she had anxiously needed to hold on to while awake fell away. The repeated nervous twitches of Muhammad's hands; the sounds of mortal combat and tinny shouts of victory in the video game; London's white coat, so big it accentuated her extreme thinness; the loud drip and splat of water drops from the tap onto the dirty dishes and utensils piled up in the sink; the Indonesian servant's dubious hand gestures; the surreptitious stares of the driver looking at her in the car's front mirror; Abdallah's unending dialogues with London and his quarrels with Salim. When she slept, she fell into a comfortable void which sent her downwards softly and gradually to where there was no longer anything. Best of all was that no dreams passed across her vision – no nightmares, no images, no voices, nothing. She savoured her enjoyable coma, a place she could go where she had nothing to confront. Sleep was her only paradise. It was her ultimate weapon against the pounding anxiety of her existence.

Now, sitting up on her bedding, Mayya heard the muezzin's voice. She found it comforting in the dawn silence. Life appeared to her sharply divided in two parts, like night and day: what we live, and what lives inside of us. She dozed off, waking up to the sound of her father opening the door, having just returned from the mosque. He squatted next to her and took the baby from her lap. Ma sha' allah, your daughter is the very picture of you, Mayya! She smiled, seeing the traces of water from his ablutions clinging to his chin, and thought about how he had no choice but to spend most of his time outside the house until she would have completed her forty days of confinement, when the women who constantly came and went would finally depart. He appeared delighted with the girl. He had already told Mayya that the baby's tiny body and sparse hair reminded him of her brother Hamad as a newborn. The dawn light edged into the room, illuminating it little by little, as Mayya and her father gazed at this new person without exchanging any more words. The rooster was crowing and she could hear the rustling of the nabk tree outside the window. Azzan returned the baby to her bed. I swear, Mayya, she really does look like Hamad! When he was born he was so tiny, only a touch larger than the palm of a hand. We said he wouldn't live but he did. And then, once he was filling our eyes with his bounce, and giving us so much joy, he left us.

Mayya could remember everything. She had been ten when it happened. Hamad was two years younger. He took off into the farmlands on his steed, which was nothing more than a dry date-palm cluster, a limb fallen from a tree, his little-boy locks of hair riffling in the breeze and the silver amulet around his neck. Together they would slip away from Qur'an school. Mayya never succeeded in mounting that stallion, though she did try to get it away from him. The date-palm branch could rip a dishdasha to shreds. But since she was a girl, she couldn't shimmy her dishdasha up her body and tie it around her middle as Hamad did his. Nor could she take it off as he sometimes did. They would steal green mangoes from Merchant Sulayman's orchard and collect unripe dates from beneath the palm trees.

Then Hamad left them. Just like that, suddenly. Mayya remembered people coming to offer condolences and mourn with them; she remembered the tears and the silver amulet. Her mother was keen to retrieve his clothes and the amulet.

No one cared about Hamad's mount. The steed remained where it was, a thin dry body splayed apart for Mayya to see, every time she stared at the base of the courtyard wall.

When her father left the room the newborn began to cry. Mayya hugged her close. Did her daughter really look like her?

Twenty-three years later when she would smash her daughter's mobile phone to bits in anger before slapping her across the face, the only remaining traces of resemblance were their brown skin and wiry frames. London would be taller than her mother, a good-looking young woman, and such a talker that it wouldn't be surprising if she were nicknamed Chatterbox. This room would have become the refuge of her grandfather, an old man in his sixties. By then, the oily blue-green, already faded, would have been covered when the room was repainted a watery light blue. Against the wall would sit modern wood wardrobes instead of her mandus, the beautiful old gilt-edged wood chest, while a sofa upholstered in velvet would have taken the place of the Indian sequined cushions. The seam where walls and ceiling joined would be hidden beneath a white strip of plaster décor and London, who no longer resembled her mother in much of anything, would not enter this room, or the house around it. Not ever. That's how afraid she was of her grandmother. But by then, this grandmother would have taken refuge in another room to which her mandus-chests had been removed along with some fancy pillows cushions, all wedged alongside the new, modern-style wood-frame bed and its accompanying suite of furniture. By then, this grandmother of hers was swearing out loud that she would slit her granddaughter's throat if the rebellious girl really did marry the peasant's son. How could she possibly marry the issue of the man who had threshed the family's grain?

Abdallah

The clouds today are very thick, impenetrable. I like the idea of being so high that gravity loses its power over me, as I stare down at the clouds. I can remember how surprised I was to learn that clouds are not substantial enough to bear a person's weight. Ustaz Mamduh exploded in laughter when he realised how deluded I was. So who do you think are, or you'll be, when you grow up? A big important man who takes off into the air and sits on top of the clouds? Those clouds are like smoke, you idiot! Only air.

A month after she graduated, London said to me, I love clouds, Papa! When I was little I used to dream I had wings, like the girl in the TV Ramadan Riddles show, and I could fly up there and sit on top of the clouds.

I did not tell her that this had been my dream too. I didn't get a chance. We were sitting in her new car. She was driving and talking incessantly. Suddenly she asked, How about we go down to the shore at Sib?

The renovations along the seafront at Sib had been completed by now, with a new coast road extending about four kilometres along that stretch of coastline. Every so often there was a stylish long asphalt parking area that allowed drivers to pause, alongside paved walkways with fancy entrelac for pedestrians, and lampposts that were miniature copies of the towering Burj al-Arab in Dubai. Long before these renovations were begun I used to go to Sib with my father, on his periodic visits to the fishermen there. He was trying to make agreements with them to buy their houses which overlooked the sea coast. He wanted to convert the area into a commercial complex. He was convinced that the Sabco and Okay Centre malls and even the al-Harthi Centre which opened during his final illness, were too far away for would-be customers who lived in the Sib area.

But the buying power here is weak, Father, I would exclaim. We are not in Dubai.

You don't understand anything about commerce! would come his response. We'll start with those fishermen, and then you'll see.

Our excursions ended, as did talk of the project, when we learned that the Ministry of Housing had prohibited such commercial ventures anywhere along the seafront. We would be in Father's white Mercedes, with me at the wheel. We didn't have anything to say to each other, unless he wanted to bring up some issue concerning his business, or to moan how sad he was that it would all very likely be lost after his passing anyway, as long as his progeny consisted of the likes of me 'who doesn't appreciate the value of a penny'. One week after his death I presented my documents to join the distance learning programme at one of the universities in Beirut. The idea was that I would travel there twice a year for the examinations, until I graduated with a BA in Business Management. It doesn't really matter to me now, Father, that you never saw my diploma. After all, you didn't have any desire to see it. But what *did* that man desire? You are my only son, he would say. I want you to be a man ... the best sort of man.

After my marriage I spent ten years on the road: back and forth between Muscat and al-Awafi. He refused to let us move to Muscat, for then who would keep the Big House alive? Who would preserve it as a home? Who would receive the guests? Who would preside over those sociable gatherings that brought men together every evening? He would not hear of it. No, no, absolutely not! We would do our business in Muscat – one day there, or perhaps two – and then we'd be back in al-Awafi. That was our home town, not Muscat. After another ten years, my son Salim said, But Muscat is our home town not al-Awafi. Why can't we spend all of our school holidays and the big feast days here in Muscat?

At first London objected to the streets in the capital city that she said were designed only for 'cars' feet'. Then she adapted herself, and she even came to like the long stretch of paved seaside corniche. But she had a response for Salim: What there is in al-Awafi that isn't in Muscat is the graveyard. Most people who live in Muscat aren't buried in Muscat. They're buried in their home villages.

On this evening she stopped her car at one of the Corniche parking areas along the Sib shoreline. She put out the lights and then she burst into sobs. I had not seen her cry even once, since her babyhood, until the year just past, on that day when her mother hit her and broke her mobile phone.

Honey, what is it? What's wrong? Is it Hanan? She will recover, my dear. She'll be all right.

London shook her head. It's not Hanan. Even though, you know, her family refused to go to court about the rape because they were afraid of the scandal, and she gave in to them.

She tugged her embroidery-edged abaya closer around her body and slouched over the steering wheel. Ahmad and I used to come here, she said. He would tell me, Don't turn around, and don't get out of the car, there are young guys running around in shorts here, don't open the window and don't look out. I would say, Ahmad, you're my love, I don't see anyone but you! He would laugh, Papa, and he'd say, Why don't you see anyone else? Are you blind or something?

When this anger overwhelms me, as it's beginning to do right now, amidst all these clouds, I don't know what to do with all of it. It won't quit, and I can't find any window for it to escape through. This anger – this rage that comes every time I picture her face as she talked, sitting there in the car. This single, fierce emotion stifles everything else, even my breathing. I have never felt so helpless in front of my anger as when my daughter was crying, and then confessing. I gave in to him, she gasped between her sobs, because I was afraid of failure.

I felt the same helpless anger when the nurse took out the tubes from my father's body, her way of announcing he was dead. This anger of mine pursues me to the edge, where I'm screaming without making the slightest sound, crying without any tears. But it's an anger that carries no force. All it accomplishes is that it keeps me from taking a breath.

I didn't feel angry when I learned, long after the event, that Zarifa had died. I just felt as though the earth had given me a violent shaking. Suddenly, I was that lone child of so long ago, whom Sanjar and Marhun forced to steal the rifle and then deprived of eating any magpies. I felt like my father was going to punish me for leaving Zarifa to die far away and alone. He would punish me, lower me into the well trussed up in the palm-frond rope. I felt her loud ringing laughter vibrating through my body, sending my whole body into shudders in the dawn. Again, I heard her whispering. Your mother did not die, my boy, no, Abdullah. Your mother is alive. The jinndjinn guarding the basil bush – they took her away, but she is alive.

I opened all the windows in the new car and listened to the sound of the waves as if that would cover up the sound of my daughter's crying. Why didn't you tell me from the start? Why did you wait a year? A whole year!

She moaned. I couldn't ... I mean, I chose him. Every one of you rejected my choice, and so I insisted. What else could I do, after that? And I was happy in the beginning. So I just tried to ignore it. And how could I possibly confess to my mother that I was wrong? What would I say to you, to any of you?

So you waited until he actually beat you. That was what it took for you to say anything?

Her sobbing got louder and I remembered her mother's wailing. He beats her? She said he beats her? The peasant's son beats my daughter, *mine*? And what kind of man beats his wife? In all of al-Awafi I have never heard of anyone beating his wife except for that old drunk Furayh. He used to come home soused and throw up on her, and then he would start hitting her. And so this educated 'dokhtoor' – as he calls himself, hah – is just another version of Furayh the drunk? He beats her? The peasant's son beats my girl? No one ever put his hand on me and no one put his hand on my mother or my sisters, and now this dog comes and beats my little girl? What a scandal we must look amongst all the tribes, every clan, our own, out in the open. The man our daughter is already legally married to, even if, thank the Lord, they haven't moved in together, and Furayh the drunk – they're cut from the same cloth? By God, if only he had never set eyes on her! By God, he's divorcing her today and he'd better do it fast.

He divorced her. We paid him the dowry and so my daughter got herself out of that marriage and got her freedom.

London, I said to her, Today you are free. You are a successful physician and you have your freedom and a good social life and he doesn't deserve even a stray thought. It was just a bad experience, it's over, and that's that.

She breathed in the sea air and left her tears rolling down her cheeks. You're right, Father. Just a bad experience.

The teenagers laugh and shout and open their cans of cola, the sea breeze grows colder, and I drive on the way back to al-Khuwayr, muttering to myself. God be praised that the actual wedding had not yet happened and the whole thing came to an end when they were still only bound by a nuptial contract.

Zarifa

Zarifa made up an enormous tray with samples of all the dishes that had been prepared for Mayya while she recovered from London's birth. A plate of rice and chicken cooked in cloves and samna; that special flatbread with honey; a tower of apples, oranges and bananas, and a ladleful of jelly-sweets. Zarifa covered the tray, balanced it on her head, and left Salima's house. She crossed the Falaj, the main canal, and then she passed the houses, the fortress-like complex where Shaykh Said and his family had lived forever, the school, and Hamdan's shop before her path brought her to the farms. In the past, al-Awafi's homes emptied completely on summer days, as everyone, young and old, converged on the farmers' fields in flight from the heat, returning home only when the soft night-time breezes wafted them there. But by this time – the early years of the 1980s – there was no need for this daily exodus. Electric fans, even air conditioners in some of the houses, put an end to these excursions. Those 'horrid new-fangled heretical air conditioners', as Zarifa called them.

Not once lifting her hand to steady the heavy tray on her head, Zarifa continued on her way, reaching the bare, uncultivated ground beyond the farms. The desert opened out before her as she walked on. She was damp with sweat but it was only a few moments before she arrived and stopped, breathing with relief. At the foot of the familiar cluster of white boulders, Zarifa lowered the tray and then knelt down beside it, wiping away her sweat with the edge of her wrap. Her loud, rough voice sailed across the rocks. Ya Baqii-ooo! Here is your food, may you give us leave to have our food, this is your share and so you can leave our share to us. Here it is, Baqiia, here's your khiratha, look, the special food of Mayya, daughter of Salima, may you leave her in peace, in her state of confinement as she heals ... may you not strike her down or harm the newborn girl.

Zarifa got back up on her feet and began the return journey to al-Awafi. Only two days before, she had undertaken this very same errand to deflect evil, but that time to ward it away from the wife of her son, also recovering from childbirth and from her own new granddaughter. Time after time she had made the same excursion. They were always successful, these offerings of hers. The jinni Baqiia had never grown angry, not once over the long period that Zarifa had dedicated herself to the jinni's service, nor in the era of her mother before her. Well, except that one time, when someone bewitched Umm Abdallah somehow while in her confinement. Before Zarifa, her mother had shouldered this duty and before that it had been her grandmother's task. All of them knew the most particular secrets about Baqiia, the jinni woman who specialised in stalking any woman recovering from childbirth who did not feed her from her own special food. Poor wretched Umm Abdallah, Zarifa muttered. May God show her His mercy, poor simple woman, she was only minding her own business. But people don't show any mercy, and this boy of hers ... well, this Abdallah, a man who's not in the caravan nor in the warring band, as the proverb-maker says. What a useless fellow, no one listens to him. What kind of man lets his wife give his daughter this strange name? But how can I say anything?

The proverb-maker said: What you criticize others for, you'll find you've got it in spades. And my son Sanjar – who named his daughter, now? By God, men no longer have any say in things. Not all men are Sulayman! Aye, wAllahi! There just aren't any Merchant Sulaymans any more. No Shaykh Saids, either. God protect you with His mercy, Mama! Where are you? Come to me, come back to your daughter and just see what the world has become.

Zarifa's mother! People had nicknamed her Khayzuran, for like a reed of bamboo she was tall and gracefully slender. Her real name was Ankabuta: Spider-Girl. Her father had been fed up with his wife's constant pregnancies and the terrible problem of finding yet another name. And the name of a baby born into a slave family must never, ever echo the names of the masters. When the time came, Spider-Girl was the only name he had in mind, and so it was.

Before she was even fifteen Ankabuta had become an ominously telling lesson for every slave woman – and every freewoman too, for that matter – who might have given even a passing thought to refusing her husband's needs. Shaykh Said imprisoned her in an ancient cell in the fortress when she refused to sleep with his slave Nasib, to whom the Shaykh had married her off. Ankabuta languished in that cell for months. Once a day her food arrived and once a night her husband arrived. People had grown very tired of hearing her scream and finally she was freed. Maybe it was because Nasib had been declaring how sick he was of always having to tie her limbs to the rusting iron bedposts and stuffing her mouth with his turban-cloth, just to get his husbandly rights.

Ankabuta came out of prison pregnant with her only daughter. She was alone when the baby came, and after tying the cord Ankabuta decided to become a midwife, competing with Sabeekah who specialised in birthing for the daughters of shaykhs. People in al-Awafi hadn't realised that Ankabuta's hard dark face concealed an awesome and voracious appetite for living, though some did have an inkling that this woman who inclined to silence and self-concealment was in fact the great Mama who presided over the zar exorcisms, once a month in the desert out beyond the fortress and the farms that marked al-Awafi's outer edges.

Abdallah

Thank you, my bright-faced air hostess. The orange cake is truly delicious even if I would have preferred our Omani jellies over any of the things you call halveh or – as London would say in emphatic English, sweeeeets. In the festival seasons or when my father's large house was filled with guests, I would always wrap up a big portion of beautifully greasy dark hilwa in a page torn from my school notebook and carry it to Ustaz Mamduh. There were many times when I didn't even get to taste these special sweets myself. In sociable gatherings the older and grander men always ate first. It was inappropriate for a young one like myself to show any appetite or to compete with the elders, and often the sweets on their tray were whisked away too rapidly for little hands like mine to have a chance. Whenever it came to that, my hopes would completely vanish, for I knew that my aunt would take charge and lock it all away in the storeroom, and I wouldn't have the courage to ask for any.

But then Zarifa remembers about Ustaz Mamduh and, before anyone can notice, spirits away a big chunk for his sake. Or for the sake of the diploma. Just seeing the green cover of my diploma told her it was something to celebrate even though she didn't understand a single word of what was written inside.

Once in a while I am enormously lucky, securing two massive chunks of it. One I wrap up for Ustaz Mamduh and the other I split with Maneen who has already caught a whiff of its light saffron smell even though I always try my hardest to keep the very scent of it under wraps. Maneen is always perched on a large rock in front of the opening to his mud house, which sits squarely on the route I have to take to school. Not a creature can pass in front of him without hearing that voice. Maneen is in bad shape, he moans. Give Maneen a few grains of rice, just a little handful! Pass him a bite of something sweet! I move from one school grade to the next but Maneen never changes his spot, as if he and the rock on which he sits were created as one piece, never to change, just as the worn-out robe he wears never changes. The only thing that changes is that he discovers mulberry cordial. He adds a line to his singsong call: Give him some Vimto to wet his throat!

Maneen's son Zayid is in my class at school but I never see Zayid with his father. He is always at school or playing with the lads in the neighbourhood. People say his mother ran off with another man when Zayid was still a nursing baby and so all the women in the neighbourhood pitched in, treating him with fondness and taking care of his needs until he was old enough to care for himself. Zayid never laughed, and when we raced he always got the better of all the other boys. Our races started where the canal begins and ended at the furthest edge of al-Awafi's farms, and Zayid was always ahead.

Whenever Maneen catches sight of me he ratchets up the musicality of his familiar call. He claps his hands together as he asks me. Soooo, Abdallah? How's your father? What little trifle have you brought poor Maneen today?

If my pockets are empty I respond by snapping at him. Maneen, I know very well that the Ministry of Welfare gives you thirty riyals! Then I take myself off, heading at a fast clip towards the school building. But if I've been lucky with my share of sweets I sit down with him on his rock and we eat the luscious jelly-like chunk together. His mouth crammed with jelly-sweets, chuckles, and saliva, Maneen repeats the same old story I have heard a thousand times. Heyyy, Abbuuud... a blessed boy just like your papa! Hooo, Abbuud, my man, in the year of the horrible rains. Kharsa! It was a disaster for sure. The water came down hard for ten whole days, this house of mine went melting into the ground and even the homes of the big folk leaked water until their roofs fell in. We were dying of hunger, my boy, the rain completely destroyed all the dates. Ruined. All of our mats and furnishings and clothing were wet through and no one could find anything to eat – nothing to buy, nothing to sell – Heyyyy, Abbuud, you came along in easy times, times of plenty. You've never seen real hunger. The year of the kharsa al-Awafi was afloat, it was just one big mess of gullies. Shaykh Said closed himself up in that fortress of his and he said to everyone, I have nothing left. All my dates have been ruined by the water, he said, and the fighting between the tribes took everything I owned.

But your father, he was a different story, bless the man! He opened his home, he put up tents for people in his own courtyard. They ate and drank until every cupboard door in the kitchen and storeroom was flung wide open and people could see with their own eyes that there was nothing more there. If it hadn't been for your father and Shaykh Masuud – God's mercy on the late Shaykh Masuud, my boy – we would have died of starvation. The year of the disaster, Abbuud – aye, and today all is fine with us, just see! The world, my son, what a world! So, Abbud – now, you don't have any Vimto for poor Maneen?

We were growing up. Zayid no longer yanked at the girls' braids without warning when we were playing hide-and-seek, dividing ourselves into two groups, boys against girls. Sanjar no longer reacted by diving for Zayid, throwing him to the ground and nearly throttling him. We grew up and Zayid went into the army. In a few years Maneen's crumbling mudbrick house disappeared from the roadside to be replaced by a reinforced concrete home, three bedrooms and a sitting room. People said that Zayid had moved up rapidly through the ranks and was much approved of by the senior staff. He came back to al-Awafi infrequently now, in his red Camry. He rebuilt the house and filled it with large sacks of rice and sugar, and sealed tins of the best local sweets, the ones from Barka. When he did show up, he was always in uniform and everyone knew he was bringing crates of fruit and bottles of Vimto. Often he had a gang of workers in tow, to build another addition or to replace the wood door with a fancier one. But Maneen, his eyesight faded and his hair gone completely white, did not abandon the small rock on which he was always perched, or his tattered clothes, or his same old cry whenever someone passed by. The neighbours could hear furious rows erupting, as ever, between the father and his army-officer son. They could hear Maneen protesting that he couldn't see any longer, and he was used to sitting by the roadside, he liked being there, it was his life, the people who came by. He didn't want to be shut up inside a house even if it was brand new! He said he was only teasing people by calling out to them. All he wanted was some amusement, the pleasure a conversation gave him. No one actually gave him anything now, as they had in the days of poverty. No one was there to wash his clothes, he said, no one to cook the rice stacked up in the house. He liked eating with the neighbours anyway, he said, he liked being in the warm damp throng of children and their games. The neighbours could not make out any of the words his son was yelling back.

When I wanted to give out alms for Muhammad's sake,

hoping he'd be cured, I went to al-Awafi and slaughtered five ewes and gave out the meat, but Maneen refused to take any of it at all. He said that if he took it and Zayid found out, he would never forgive him. The Indian woman whom Zayid brought to the house as a servant tried to help Maneen undress and clean himself. She kept at it for a few weeks but then she started spending all of her time on her own needs. When her belly swelled up enough that no one could possibly ignore her state any longer, Zayid came and got her and sent her back to her own country. Maneen returned to his old ways and his usual appearance, the cheerful dirty face, his laughter and his stone perch. His calls came now in a faded voice that was hard to hear. Or he went silent, withdrawing inside his cement house, especially whenever Zayid was in al-Awafi.

Maneen yells out: The year of the disaster, my boy! Sanat al-kharsa, it was. When the water came pouring over the land, green places and dry brown ones both. But praise be to God, we lived through it. We huddled in the tents at your papa's place, all crowded together, and at Shaykh Masoud's, too, dividing up the dates and the dried fish, ten to a plate. Ilhamdulillah! Heyy, Abbuud, you're sure you don't have a swallow of Vimto anywhere in the house? You say to me, the pension from the Ministry. Thirty riyals, Abbud, that won't even pay for a cig, so how is it supposed to pay for the notebooks and pens Zayid needs? Hafiza! Well, you see, it costs three riyals just to give her a look. She'll say, Go take a shower, Maneen, and then you can come to me here. May God provide for the women, they've got no other way. In the year of the horrible rains, my boy, the women were dying of hunger, and one of them would sell herself even for half a penny. But some of them, well, Abbud, they were a stubborn bunch, money wouldn't do it and neither would pretty words. I brought this Hafiza a bottle of Vimto as big around as my forearm is, and she still wasn't satisfied. She didn't taste hunger, she didn't see the year of the horrible rains. She'd say, Go wash yourself, go on now ... Now I ask you, is Zaatar any better than me?

Years later, when his eyesight was gone and his teeth falling out, Maneen joined in at the zar exorcisms, walking over hot coals and screaming as much as he pleased. The night he was found dead, from a rifle shot to his head, he had returned from the zar very late and very drunk. For hours after he returned, he was shouting, standing there in front of the door to his house. Poor Maneen! Wretched Maneen! Give him a bite of bread, give him a half-cigarette, give him a woman even if it is only filthy Hafiza!

Some folks said he'd simply been a wretched murder victim, they even called him a martyr, and they prayed over him. But others called him an immoral drunkard and would not join the prayers. They hoisted his body and did a proper burial procession, taking him to the graveyard west of al-Awafi. When the police arrived the next morning, no one claimed to know anything. No, they hadn't heard a thing. In a few days the case file was closed. And no one in al-Awafi saw Zayid ever again.

Teacher Mamduh taught us in all subjects. There were no girls in our class. But between classes, Zayid would steal to the first-year group where four girls studied along with the boys. He would single out one of the four, pull her hair and run off. Finally Khawla complained about him to her father Azzan. After that, he had to stop.

When we were studying the Chapter of the Back-biter from the Qur'an, Zayid would glance sidelong at me whenever we launched into reciting those particular verses: 'Beware the back-biter, who piles up riches as he piles up the faults of others, counting his wealth and bad-mouthing others, but will his hundreds give him eternal life?' Teacher Mamduh went into long and elaborate detail, cursing the rich and their accumulation of wealth, and the merchants who hoarded gold. All the while, Zayid's flame-throwing glances were burning me alive. And so, on the day when Ustaz Mamduh asked us what our fathers did for a living – when he already knew perfectly well what the answers would be – I almost died of embarrassment. I didn't have the courage to say that mine was a merchant. The boys said, easily and confidently: He's a farmer ... a blacksmith ... farmer ... carpenter ... men's dishdasha tailor ... judge ... muezzin ... farmer ... while I broke out in a sweat, afraid to call out that my papa was a merchant. I had the uncomfortable feeling that the word *merchant* meant a fat ugly disgusting person with a bulging belly which jiggled and swayed as he piled up gold and tortured the poor. I was sure that my secret as the son of a rich man – he owned what was only the second automobile in all of al-Awafi, after Shaykh Said's – would be revealed and then I would be the butt of some truly mean taunts. Just then Zayid shouted, His papa is Merchant Sulayman! The owner of the Big House, and the farms, and his land goes all the way to Maskad.

No one mocked me but I felt ashamed, like I myself was in disgrace. I wished hard that my father was a farmer like most of the boys' fathers were.

In the break, Zayid and I were the only boys in the class who did not go to the canteen because neither of us had any spending money. Until I reached middle school, my father was absolutely firm; there was no way he was going to give me a hundred pennies every day for school. By the time I was finally given this allowance, other people were giving their children two or three hundred. I always had to choose between bread, cheese or a carton of Suntop juice drink. I couldn't have both or all of them at the same time. Not until the very end of high school.

Masouda

Although the neon streetlamps confidently signalled the route to every house in al-Awafi, on the rough road to Masouda's house they flickered, hesitant. Her senses picked up the grinding rasp of the rusty iron door as soon as anyone would begin pushing it open to step over the threshold. The narrow packed-dirt courtyard led one into a cramped semi-circular space and a tiny room whose door didn't close properly. The walls were lined with images on thin, dog-eared paper of the Grand Mosque in Mecca and the Prophet's Mosque in Medina, and one luridly coloured image in a wood frame of Buraq, the heavenly steed who carried the Prophet skyward, an elegant creature portrayed with a beautiful feminine countenance. Thin mattresses – just cheap fabric stretched over a layer of sponge – were propped against the wall next to an assortment of plastic implements: baskets of various sizes and colours, big ladles, and pots with white lids. Next to the open door was a mirror in an ancient frame at the top of which was written in pyramidal form 'Sultanate of Muscat and Oman'. The sitting room was completely empty but for a carpet whose edges were partly worn away and a rolled-up mat that always stood in the corner. But Masouda hadn't set foot in any of these spaces for a long time. One of the women who lived nearby might stop in at midday, or a young boy or two at sunset. As the iron door scraped open groaning, the smell that had been imprisoned inside burst out. Masouda would shout, I'm here! I'm here . . . and anyone around would truly know she was indeed *there*.

At the furthest point to the right from the courtyard was a tiny room – once used as a threshing floor – with a toilet attached which was nothing more than a crack the length of the dirt floor with a metal pitcher next to it. Ever since her daughter had announced that Masouda was mad, the old woman had been confined in the tiny room furnished only with a reed mat covering the pebbles. She improvised a makeshift window from an opening in the wall where three metal skewers formed bars and a wooden shutter hung. There was nothing in the room other than the column to which Masouda would be tied when her screams were at their loudest and she seemed almost ready to smash open the locked wooden door by throwing her body against it. Whenever she heard the low screech of the door she would grip the window bars desperately and shout, I'm in here! I'm Masouda and I'm in here!

Twice each day her daughter Shanna came in with lunch and dinner, from the home of Merchant Sulayman. She almost never opened her mouth in response to Masouda's cries as she handed her mother the heaping plate and took the empty one. A neighbour woman might come by, earning herself a good deed by stopping sometimes beneath the barred window for a chat. The young boys from the village crept in periodically to relieve themselves at the foot of the wall or to threaten Masouda if she didn't stop screaming so loudly.

Now and then Shanna showed up for an unexpected visit, looking in on her mother, filling the pitcher in the toilet. Exactly a fortnight into each month she gave her mother a bath, washed and plaited her hair, swept the place out and sprinkled water across the dirt courtyard.

I am Masouda! I am Masouda and I'm in here …

On some days the breeze was vigorous enough to budge the rusty metal door. It wasn't Shanna or a neighbour woman or the boys, but without any lamp, how could Masouda know to stop shouting as long and as loud as she could?

I'm in heeeeere! I am Masouda …

Abdallah

Salim worries me. After his poor showing in the high school exams, one of the private colleges did give him a place but even that was difficult to secure. I'm not pleased with anything that boy does or who he is.

London says to me, Negative! You are just so negative, Dad! Soon she will really turn into a mature grown-up. Now that she can regain some peace of mind after her bad love affair, she'll start a new page. How happy I feel when I see her smile, on her way to the hospital, pulling on her doctor's coat. Praise be to God who has blessed humankind with the ability to forget!

As a little boy I got used to hearing Habib suddenly bark, Forgetting? Where is it, this forgetting? I never liked Habib, not at all. Whenever he saw me with Zarifa he gave me a shove. He knew I wouldn't dare tell my father. Zarifa never defended me when it happened. I was very happy when Habib disappeared for good. His son Sanjar was no more than six when people started whispering that Habib had escaped. Habib's ancient mother screamed and rolled herself madly in the sand and tore her clothes to shreds. She seemed to know, somehow, that he would never come back. But it didn't surprise anyone to find him gone. He was always saying that he would go back to that land from which he'd been snatched away, back to his freedom, plundered by pirates and merchants. Some years later, someone said they'd caught a glimpse of him in the Baluch Café in Dubai – that was when every nation had their own café there – but others were certain he really had gone back to Makran, in Baluchistan, that he'd married and had children there. Still others said he had died of tuberculosis not long after escaping, and before the change in regime that brought with it a rush of new hospitals.

Zarifa didn't shed one tear over him and I never heard her talk about him. Once when I was older I asked her why she didn't try to find anything out about him. She answered with her favourite line. The proverb-maker says: Knowledge means pain, not knowing keeps me sane. But raising Sanjar, she couldn't keep him ignorant. When he had grown up and had children, he emigrated to Kuwait. She didn't roll in the sand or tear her clothes to rags, though. She waited eight years, until my father was dead, and then she went after her son. Very soon she was back, spitting and swearing at *the viper* whom her son had married. After that, I had no more news of her. I was completely preoccupied with the nosedive in the market, with real estate, with building the new house in Muscat, with London's marriage and divorce, Salim's studies and Muhammad's illness, and all the worries of the world. Then I heard suddenly that Zarifa had died.

I went to my father's funeral after he died in hospital. When my uncle died of a heart attack, and Zayd drowned in the flood, and Maneen was killed by a bullet, and Hafiza died of AIDS and Marwan killed himself with his father's dagger, I went to their funerals, and I also attended funerals for my friends' fathers and mothers, but I didn't go to Zarifa's. Simply, no one told me. She got ill without my knowing and she died and was buried and I still didn't know.

I saw my father in my dreams, his eyes red from so much anger. He was brandishing a palm-fibre rope in my face as he asked me about her. Ahh, Habib! Your mother is very old, but she is still alive, even now. Where are you, and your shouts into my childish face? Forgetting? Where is this place called Forgetting?

Mayya and London

The visitors are giving their full attention to the sweets and fruits. Zarifa pours out coffee for the women and doesn't let a sentence go by without commenting on it. Laughter rises, voices mingle, repeating complaints about husbands and children, news of marriage, divorce, and recent childbirths, commentary on the startlingly bright fabrics flooding Hamdan's shop, the televisions whose presence was no longer limited to the homes of Shaykh Said and Merchant Sulayman, or which mudbrick house had most recently been replaced by a cement-block rectangle. They had things to laugh about, and their hostess, Salima, smiled to show that she shared their good cheer.

Yesterday – and for the first time ever in her married life – Azzan had given her a gold ring that held an enormous blue stone. Everyone knew Salima despised gold and scorned any sort of adornment. What she had been obliged to buy as a bride she had kept in a locked steel box buried deep inside her large wooden wedding chest. She and Azzan had never exchanged gifts. He always gave her what she needed and he never asked her about household expenses: but gifts were another story! Salima felt uneasy about her husband's impulsive offering.

As she disappeared into the kitchen to prepare more fruit, the muezzin's wife and Judge Yusuf's widow bent their heads together to whisper. Sister, what kind of man is Abdallah, allowing his daughter to have this odd name? Seems he doesn't get to say a word about it, doesn't his woman Mayya listen to him? If he had any balls, if he could make her listen, he would never have left it to her to name the girl for a city in the land of the Christians. London! Since when does anyone name his daughter after a place anyway?

Mayya eats dates alone in bed. Asma's attempts to convince her mother that they should always eat together had fizzled. The prophetic hadiths she recited had no effect but to anger Muezzin-Wife, who accused her of deliberately attempting to revise the faith and corrupt it with evil innovations from books. None of this bothered Mayya. She wasn't particularly concerned about food and whether she consumed it in others' company or not. She did not understand how women could spend so much time eating and talking. She, on the other hand, was silently watching her little daughter make a tiny triangle with her lips, and open and close her eyes. London's crying lessened and she began spending longer periods batting at the air with her hands and feet. Mayya loved watching her swatting at the air, but her mother insisted on swaddling the baby. Mayya had chosen the white swaddling herself from Ruwi Souq when she'd gone to Muscat to give birth. She also bought tiny white undershirts and two little yellow gowns that would suit either a boy or a girl perfectly well. She hid Khawla's lipstick among her clothes, hoping her mother wouldn't spot it.

She didn't know what it was that worried her mother so much about Khawla. Mayya saw her as a gentle person, quick to sympathise with others, the prettiest and sweetest girl in al-Awafi. What was the problem if she insisted that her father buy her a ring and some gold bangles? She deserved them, and her father could afford it. Mayya was uncomfortable when her mother attacked Khawla for what seemed the most trivial of reasons. If her mother didn't like jewellery, that was her business, but couldn't she let Khawla alone? If only London would turn out as pretty as her aunt!

Mayya sighed and looked closely at her tiny daughter's black hair which had slowly begun to grow. Her gaze settled on the baby's forehead, slightly more wrinkled than it should be, she thought. She asked herself whether it was true that a person's fate was written on their brow, as people always said. What was written on the tiny forehead of this new little creature?

How could Mayya have seen, on her baby daughter's brow, the evenings of sleeplessness that would come as she reached her early twenties, all of those nights to come when Ahmad's face visited London insistently before his features faded so completely that she began doubting he was a real person with whom she had had a real relationship, that they had actually met, then also that they had really and truly broken up. London would try to hold his image in her mind but at the same time to banish it. It was usually just before dawn that her memory would bring up a certain image, always the same one, the portrait published in the university magazine. She saw something in that image that she hadn't noticed in person. In the photo, his eyes shifted away from the camera. Eventually London had understood that look as one she could not trust.

Mayya stroked her daughter's forehead and touched her wiry hair. Early in the morning Abdallah came in to see her, bringing cases of baby food in little jars. Mayya found this unnecessary and slightly disgraceful, but she didn't say anything. First of all, this brand-new baby girl wouldn't eat actual food for at least three months. Second, it wasn't as if she, Mayya, was incapable of cooking for her daughter and had to have him bring her jars of Heinz and Milupa which had been canned only God knew when. No one in al-Awafi fed their babies such things. If he thought she was going to imitate his uncle's wife in Maskad he was wrong. Mayya did not speak much but she would not imitate anyone. She would cook, herself, for her daughter. She would sew her daughter colourful frocks that no one had seen the like of on a little girl before. This girl would never leave the house without her hair combed and shoes on her feet and a frock with long bold stripes down the middle. Mayya would really prove now how truly skilled she was at sewing. London's clothes would not look like anyone else's just as her name echoed no other girl's.

Abdallah

On the day we moved to the new house I saw my mother in a dream. I saw her wrapped in a long, loose-fitting white garment, walking over the water. I was walking behind her and calling out. Mama, Mama! But she did not turn around for me and I did not see her face until I woke up. I wish cameras had reached al-Awafi before she died. Zarifa always told me that I looked like her, though my paternal aunt was constantly insisting that I looked like my father.

The day London got the divorce she asked Ahmad for, and we returned the dowry, I saw my mother in a dream again. I saw her walking calmly ahead of me. I was gripping the hem of her veil and saying, Mama, why did you pull up the basil shrub? But she did not turn around for me. I didn't hear her voice.

When I learned that Zarifa had died I saw my father first in a dream and then I saw her, tall and thin. She hugged me tightly. I was very short, barely reaching her middle, and she bent over me. Her hug was Mayya's and her face was Zarifa's.

As usual I found Mayya asleep. When we all stay up talking in the evening, she leaves to go to sleep as soon as my conversations with London or with Salim grow tense. When I come home from work in the late afternoon more often than not I find Mayya asleep.

Way back when I was a boy, if I ever dozed in the late afternoon Zarifa would fume. She would shout at me. The proverb-maker says: Quarrel with your neighbour if you must to make your mark, but never ever nap before dark! Mayya never formed the kind of serious bonds with neighbours that one would have to have even to quarrel, and she would drop off to sleep whenever she chose.

In the first years of our marriage she always woke up early and almost never took afternoon naps. After Muhammad was born, you could measure her sleep with his years. At first she would go to sleep beside him in that narrow little bed of his; even later on, once he had gotten older and his body filled the bed, she would lay down with him though then she would leave him on his own. Many times, when I came home in the evening I found them lying together on the bed, gazing at the ceiling where the electric fan spun. Muhammad was completely fixed on watching the fan move. If it stopped he would start crying, and he wouldn't stop. So of course we kept the fan turning no matter what the temperature was. Mayya stayed in bed lying at his side for hours on end until he dropped off to sleep and she could leave him, to sleep herself.

Husbands

Salima spoke to her daughters about it. Asma, Khawla, look here! She told them that Emigrant Issa's two sons, who were in town now, had asked for the two of them. Khalid and Ali wanted to marry the sisters. She and their father Azzan could find no reason to turn them down, she informed them.

Asma was unruffled. She would think about it, she told her mother coolly. But she instructed her parents not to respond before she informed them of her own decision.

But Khawla, listening to her mother and sister, dropped her jaw, unable to hide her astonishment. When they were finally silent, she began saying *no*, faintly at first but then fiercely. No, no, no, no. They had never seen Khawla like this, never seen this semi-hysterical edge to her personality. She ran toward the girls' room at the other end of the courtyard and shut the door behind her. She refused to open up to anyone before her father's return. She would talk to him herself.

Asma continued as usual, helping her mother in the kitchen and in all the duties of the household, making coffee every morning and in the late afternoon for the women who were always visiting, dandling her sister's nursing baby, discussing books with Mayya, listening to the radio, reading, and washing clothes for her father, for her sister just out of childbirth, and for the baby, the constant nappies of the newborn girl. But not for a moment could she stop thinking about this engagement. A few days later she said to her mother, just offhand as she was pounding cardamom seeds for coffee, Mama, okay, fine, I will accept this Khalid boy.

As she spoke, Azzan was hurrying home. He had returned unusually late from the Bedouin settlement. The cold wind slapped at his clothes. The recent events in his life had tugged him hither and yon, until he no longer knew where he was. Insinuations and sly suggestions seemed to meet him at every turn. The day before, swapping instantly-composed lines of poetry in playful competition with his daughter as they often did, Asma had disobeyed the rules of the game. He had declaimed

The beloved's face gives yours more beauty
The more you give it your gaze

Asma shot back two separate lines in response, openings to famous poems by the ancient poet al-Samau'al and the 'Abbasid poet al-Buhturi, but neither was composed on the same rhyme scheme, as they should have been, in the spirit of the game.

If a person's honour is not sullied by base acts
then every garment he dons is beauteous

and then

I guarded myself from what would soil my self
and held myself above the paltry offerings of the scoundrel

So were people sensing Qamar's presence in him? This beautiful Moon, Najiya? This wondrous Qamar had taught him his own body, as though he'd been completely clueless about it always before. This Qamar had taught him enticements that shattered his old existence to pieces. The way he felt about it, he hadn't known anything at all about anything before he knew her. Every evening when his feet sank into the sand as he hurried toward the fragrance of her, whether he wanted it or not his whole being was driving him to this presence that was so extraordinary and had transformed his life. Coming to meet her like this simply intensified his thirst.

From the start they shared a clear sense of what this was. A free relationship. Freedom, yes, in this bond they had made. At first it did really seem that they had climbed to the summit of pure desire, free of artificiality, concealment, or deception. Between themselves, anyway. No promises made, no aspirations hinted, just each moment's blaze of passion. No ties from the past and more important, no ties to the future. That's what they wanted and worked for. A few weeks later Azzan discovered that this free relationship was collapsing into the roughest and most violent sort of slavery, driven by need, binding them in irons. It distracted him from everything else, as he saw this unending cycle of union and separation enveloping them, slaves to a vicious cycle of never-ending demands and doubts. His need for her was profound, as violent and as obscure, too, as it seemed, all the more so when he was actually with her. But now, reaching home, Azzan opened the massive wood door calmly, thinking, That's the way it is. There's no freedom in love, and you can't choose – others are there, or they're not. He walked through the courtyard without noticing the lamp lit in the girls' room. Entering the sitting room, he found everyone there, alert and tense, waiting for him to come home. Except for Khawla.

Cocooned in a big green wool shawl, Mayya was nursing her baby girl. Asma was with her, patting the newborn girl's swaddling into place, and avoiding raising her head. Salima was hunched over, but in her crouching posture she still glared at him. He took off his shoes and sand dribbled from his toes. She did not stand up and come over as she usually did. He rubbed at his beard once or twice and asked, What's going on?

Your daughter Khawla shut herself up this morning and refused to talk to anyone until you were back, Salima said. Azzan put his shoes back on and returned to the courtyard. He knocked softly on the door to his daughters' room.

Salima sighed. A puff of cold breeze, a gentle brief rain pour. Winter reminded her of her childhood, though when she remembered childhood she felt a thin thread of bitterness wrapping tightly around her heart. She was floating in a soft gloomy cloud; no, she was lying on jagged rock. She saw her father. She always saw him in two images that came to her in a dream. He was bending over her, drops of cold ablution water dripping from his beard, to hoist her onto his shoulder, with her brother Muaadh on his other shoulder. In the other image he aged and then died, all in a cold winter. Salima hated the wintertime. It seemed to carry the smell of the rough wool blanket and the sheet that shrouded her father, and also the coals that warmed the room where he was dying.

Khawla's eyes were puffy, her nose bright red. Her father had betrayed her, she sobbed. Betrayed his promise to his brother on his brother's deathbed, and now he meant to sell her off to Ali, son of the Emigrant. How could anyone think of coming to engage her when she was already engaged? How could her father even consider the idea of accepting this suitor and betraying her late uncle?

Khawla talked and talked. She would never stop talking, she said to her father, the way Mayya had stopped talking when they married her off without anyone asking her opinion. Mayya had not had an education but Khawla had, and she would kill herself if her father insisted on this marriage. She was vowed to her cousin, the son of her late uncle, and he was equally vowed to her and no creature on earth had a right to overlook this fact.

Azzan listened to his daughter until she had said all she had to say. It hurt badly, listening to her and knowing how little he had gotten to know this daughter who was barely sixteen but knew herself well enough to want to kill herself for the sake of a cousin who no one had heard from for several years.

Khawla, try not to worry, he said to her. It will be all right. He left the girls' room and returned to the sitting room. He did not stop or turn to speak to anyone, but continued on, into his own room. The rain stopped and Azzan lay wide awake until morning.

Abdallah

My uncle's wife stood in the courtyard of her modern poured-cement home in Wadi Aday. Hands planted on her hips, she screeched at me. Your father raised you with an iron fist and it certainly didn't do you any good! You can't even raise a finger to name your own daughter, huh? Loondoon! This name – what is it? I don't seem to recall seeing anyone naming his girl baby al-Awafi or Matrah or Nizwa or Wadi Aday.

I felt a laugh coming on but I managed to suppress it. My cousin Marwan, who was also known as the Pure, was sitting on the bench just inside the entry to the courtyard and gazing at us, not saying a word. Marwan was always silent, unlike his brother Qasim who was closer to me in age. So I was partial to the littler Marwan, to his silent wanderings and the way he lost himself in thought. I didn't say anything to my uncle's wife, who had browbeaten my uncle years before to get him to move the family away from al-Awafi out of fear of my father's heavy hand. My uncle's wife sold that house in Wadi Aday surrounded by tiny shops after my uncle's death. My uncle's wife did not return the corpse of Marwan the Pure to al-Awafi to be buried in the graveyard there, where everyone else was buried.

I didn't actually hate my uncle's wife. When I was small

she lived with my uncle and their children in the north wing of our house but she insisted on doing her own cooking for her children while she left my uncle to share our food. All the time, I heard the sounds of quarrelling between her and the sister of my father and uncle, and my uncle's attempts to reconcile them. I would be sitting on the bench next to our front door after the dawn prayer when she passed by, a bundle of laundry balanced on her head, going to the falaj. It was a rare occasion when she turned to speak to me and then it was always to ask the same question: What did you have for dinner last night? I would never answer. It embarrassed me. Talking about food was considered shameful in our house. If I were to ask Zarifa, What are you making for lunch? the only response I would get would be, You'll see. That was the way it was with food in our home. We saw it when it was in front of us, and we ate it quickly without any conversation, washed our hands and thanked God and didn't say a word, and heaven forbid we criticise anything! But my uncle's wife asked me this strange question, so odd when she must know that our house – packed as it was with slaves and guests at every meal – was not the kind of place where food could remain a secret. Why would anyone ask about it? If it wasn't rice with lamb and spices it was fish with onions and lemon and dried sardines. So much was certain.

One day I sat watching the other children playing ball. I was hoping to get in there with them but my father had forbidden me to leave the house unless I was with him. My heart leapt with every goal and I would scream, GOOOAAAL! as I jumped up from the bench. My uncle's wife came outside, the water from the bundle of newly washed clothes running down into her hair and her body a mass of energy and balance. Seeing me, she laughed. Did someone tie you up here, my boy? And then: What did you have to eat last night? I jumped up so fast, and I was so close to her, that I knocked the wet clothes she was carrying out of her grip and they tumbled onto the dirt as I shouted, Poison! We ate poison, are you happy? The sparks flew from her eyes, but Masouda came at just the right moment and hustled me away.

Masouda was panting under the load of firewood on her back after spending the early dawn hours in the desert outside the farms of al-Awafi, breaking off dried branches from the acacia trees and wrapping them in bundles. Later in the day she would turn this firewood into coals that could be set beneath the cauldrons that held our dinner. Early the next morning she would be out there again, bending low to pick up a new bundle of firewood. Don't speak to her, she said to me, panting. Come on, come inside. From that day on, my uncle's wife ignored me completely and a few months later she took my uncle and the children and they settled in Wadi Aday in the capital city.

I didn't hear that question about what we were having for dinner ever again, until I grew up and travelled. Then, I discovered that people would talk for hours about their food. Television ads showing open mouths happily consuming various dishes shocked me. Around me, people asked each other in all simplicity, What did you have to eat? Or, What are you going to have for dinner? My son Salim returns from college and before he says Good evening he asks, What's for supper? If his mother's response doesn't please him he turns around and leaves the house, heading for the pizza takeout or McDonald's.

Khawla

As soon as her father left the room Khawla hurried to the door, pulling it tightly shut as it had been before. She stood leaning against the window, breathing heavily. It took her a moment to notice that the rain was coming down hard, and then she sat down on the floor, her face toward where Mecca would be. Her mother had always said that your prayers are especially powerful when rain is coming down. Lifting her hands high, she repeated the same supplication that she uttered at the end of every set of prayers, and whenever it rained, and when she was fasting. O Lord, bring Nasir back to me. Bring him back before I die of grief.

She rested her head on the open palm of her right hand and curled up in the foetal position. She loved listening to the sound of the rain, and she loved even more running beneath it and feeling the wetness seeping all the way into the roots of her hair. Just then, though, she knew she wouldn't dare go anywhere near the sitting room if she were to go out into the rain first, and there was no real way to hide. One way or another, her mother would catch sight of her. If she were to go outside, it would even be difficult to slip by unnoticed into the girls' room to dry herself off before someone saw her. She turned onto her back and stared at the ceiling, the white fan, and the neon strip, her mind on Nasir.

When they were little, they had played together every afternoon with the other neighbourhood children. They formed teams: one from the eastern quarter and the other from the western quarter, each team chasing the other through all the little streets and dead-end alleys of al-Awafi. Khawla always tried to avoid Zayid because he was forever catching hold of her braids and yanking them. She stayed close to Nasir wherever he went. Most often, the two of them slipped away from the collective tag game. Nasir would dart over to the muezzin's house to pluck a red rose from the lone rosebush in the courtyard. He would poke it into her braid but he always forgot her words of caution: Take the thorn off the stem first! More than once a rose from the muezzin's house scarred her forehead.

Khawla turned onto her side, laying her head on her left palm, with the one picture on the wall staring at her. Mayya had hung it there before she left this room to get married. A thin gilt frame enclosed a broad pasture, the green grass extending into the distance and massed clouds overhead. Of course there was no such thing in the world! Mayya always protested that there was, in England. All of these enormous green spaces? How could that possibly be? The biggest expanse of green Khawla had ever seen was their farm, where she'd hid the envelope containing Nasir's picture by shoving it into the split in the palm-tree trunk.

Her memory of that day was vivid. As the light began to fade, the group of boys and girls were tiring of their games, and most headed home. Nura proposed another game that they sometimes played: Names and Jobs. Each child wrote out a list of names, numbered, and likewise of jobs. Then each chose a number, and that would yield the name of a future husband or wife, and a job. When Abd al-Rahman,

Judge Yusuf's son, chose number twenty, Khawla was the name that came up. Nasir said, Change your number! Abd al-Rahman refused. Nasir got angry and fought with him, leaving his nose bloody, all the while yelling, Khawla is my cousin and my wife, mine, we are engaged!

How old had she been when that happened? She could not have been more than nine. And Nasir? Perhaps twelve, or maybe even thirteen. She remembered how he had led her by the hand to his home where her uncle's widow offered her dates in clarified butter, and how, before she left, he had pressed the envelope into her hand. Inside was his picture, which he had torn off his school certificate. She remembered, too, how her mother beat her when she returned so late, darkness already filling the world around her.

Khawla turned onto her back, interlocking her fingers beneath her neck. She did not much like this glossy milky blue paint that the room had been covered in but even so, it was a room where she could feel at ease. Mayya was no longer a little girl when her mother began talking about adding a special room for the sisters, one that did not open onto the other rooms and that especially remained apart from the sitting room. Their home was *madkhul* as her mother always said – a house people flocked to, a house that was always full of others. Women were always coming and going, and especially, sitting and visiting in the big room. These girls were getting older, their womanhood was beginning to blossom, and their mother wanted to keep them invisible to her visitors' ever-curious eyes. Anyway, their mother knew, it simply would not do for these growing girls to hear the conversations the older women were always having, which Salima referred to as women's foolishness.

Khawla and her sisters welcomed the idea. A room at the other end of the courtyard would mean Asma could be alone with her books, as she preferred, and Khawla with her mirror, as she liked. As for Mayya, usually she did her sewing in the sitting room, anyway, except when it was filled with women and her mother signalled that she must leave. She must go to the girls' room. Khawla sighed. That was before Mayya had gotten married. Since then she had begun to share in the women's gatherings, bringing her scrawny little one with her.

A large red carpet covered much of the room. Lined up against one side of the wall stood three wooden wardrobes, one apiece. Her mother had gone to the carpenter to order them specially, choosing the dimensions and the decorative carvings for them herself. That is why Khawla didn't have a wardrobe with a mirror the height of the door. In fact, the only mirror she had was this small rectangle in its thin wood frame hanging on the wall facing the wardrobes. She had to stand tall to comb her hair or to apply the new lipstick that Mayya had managed to get for her in Muscat. On their wedding night, what would Nasir say when he saw how long and soft her hair was now?

Asma's books spilled over from her shelves onto Mayya's shelves now, because she had so many of these books. Khawla was astonished at how oblivious Asma seemed to the awful boredom these ancient books induced. The only books Khawla could bear to read were translations of Harlequin Romances, books that Asma scorned, refusing to be seen holding them for even a few moments.

Her friend Nura had discovered these novels on a visit to her relatives in Muscat. She brought a few to Khawla, who was soon addicted. These books were beautiful stories about love and they always took place in forests or green pastures or verdant plains. The heroine always had a delicate prettiness and the hero was always strong and handsome and noble. Lying in bed before she dropped off to sleep, Khawla would imagine herself with Nasir on that remote and lush island she had read about in one of these novels, the two of them surrounded by animals and birds and the magical sounds of nature. Nasir's photograph remained in her wardrobe, concealed among the folds of her clothes, for several months, before Nura warned her that her mother might stumble across it. They agreed that the best spot for it was the biggest palm-tree trunk on her father's farm. There the picture lay stuffed inside its envelope in the tree trunk, hidden by the palm fronds. Khawla made her pilgrimages to that tree throughout the years of adolescence. That day, when her uncle's widow disappeared into the kitchen to get the dates and samna, Nasir grabbed her hand and said, Don't ever marry Abd al-Rahman! You are engaged to me. I am the son of your uncle, after all, not him.

Khawla did not forget Nasir's words. Certainly Nasir could not have forgotten them either. Two years, or three, or five, who cared! So what if his circumstances had kept him from returning? He must be very busy with his studies, and he couldn't send letters to Khawla out of fear of her mother's anger. Of course not. He hadn't forgotten her. She was engaged to him, and she would wait for him.

When Nasir passed his secondary school examinations and cans of soda pop were handed round to the neighbours to celebrate the occasion, Khawla was still in middle school. Deliriously happy, she drained three entire cans of soda all by herself. She gave him an eye-catching silver pen that Nura had bought for her in Muscat. As she looked on, he kissed the pen, and she was so embarrassed she almost hoped the earth would open and swallow her up. He told her he had gotten a scholarship to Canada, and she should start now to prepare for the wedding, which they would have the next summer, then he could take her back there with him. She cried, and she drew red hearts pierced by arrows on the long letter she wrote, and when she found she had no picture of herself to give him (that's what the heroines in romance novels always did), she imitated what he had done years before. She tore the photo off her sixth grade school certificate and gave it to him. It was an old picture; what he saw was a dazed-looking little girl in long braids with a blue amulet hanging protectively round her neck.

Lying on the red carpet, Khawla tossed restlessly and moaned. The rumours whirling around refused to disappear. People said Nasir had failed his first year; they said he had gotten involved in things that had nothing to do with study and couldn't get out; they said he wasn't in touch with anyone here now, not even his mother; they said the Ministry in Muscat had cut off his scholarship money because time after time he had failed his exams. They said he would not be coming back. Well, let them say whatever they wanted! Nasir would come back. He would come back to her, to pretty Khawla who had waited for him, who still waited for him, always taking good care of herself, preserving her looks for his sake and the sake of their upcoming marriage.

The brown plastic bank moulded into the form of a house sat on the shelf in her wardrobe. No one knew it was a gift from him, on the day she passed her first year of middle school. Every time she dropped a hundred bisa into the slot that bisected its roof, Khawla swore that the money would reappear only to pay the costs of their wedding. So then, who was this son of Emigrant Issa who dared to try to win her hand? Didn't he know that she was already engaged? How could he be so insultingly bold? And how could they engage her to someone when she already had a first cousin and was vowed to him?

WAllahi wAllahi wAllahi! May my throat be slit, my neck carved like a lamb, sliver by sliver, if my family insists on marrying me to the son of Emigrant Issa. I will kill myself, I swear to God I will.

Abdallah

Through the airplane window I see streams of light far below, spilling from cities along the coastline to arc into the sea. The flows of light follow a quiet, meandering course, not at all like the fierce spills of water in al-Awafi that drowned Zayd.

The floods came about a year before I first saw Mayya at her sewing machine. The image of Zayd's body swollen by floodwaters haunted me, chasing me through every dream I had. Returning home on those evenings when I had stolen away to hear the wails of Suwayd's oud, I would find Zayd's ghost looming in front of me all of a sudden, blocking my way. It was only when I saw Mayya, so sad and pretty and pale, bending over the sewing machine as if she were putting her arms around a tiny child, that I stopped seeing Zayd, whether in my dreams or on the dark path leading back to my father's house.

I came out of my heavy moods. In the melodies and rhythms of Suwayd's oud I could almost feel myself dwindling to nothing, a little like the way I sensed myself dissolving in the cloudy pallor of Mayya's face. Perhaps I came close to becoming a fast-moving little stream myself, a rush of water ready to sweep away the sewing machine and plant me in its place. I could nearly feel my own earliest, inchoate self, my flesh recreated in Mayya's thin fingers on the fabric, in Suwayd's thin fingers stretched over the strings of his instrument.

If only my father had not caught sight of me.

For some reason he hadn't stayed in his room as he usually did after the evening prayers. Having assumed that he'd sought the refuge of his bed as he did every night, I went out and Zarifa locked the door behind me. We both knew she would unlock it before going to sleep.

But when I returned I found the door bolted. I stood there confused and afraid. Did it make sense that Zarifa would forget about me? Or had some other person come along after her and locked the door?

My bewilderment didn't last long. The door whipped open and I saw my father's face through the darkness.

Fattum's boy ... yes, Fattum's son. So you think you're grand enough to go against me, d'you? Me? You'd disobey me? Fattum's son! He bellowed a lot of words at me, most of which I didn't understand or even hear – except my mother's name. I lost consciousness after a blow somewhere to my head. He left me bleeding, lying in front of the gate. When I came to, I could hear Zarifa weeping but I couldn't see her.

When he had kicked me, I yelled. I am not a boy any longer! I screamed my rage in his direction. And I will go out at night to have some fun. Like any other guy my age.

But in fact, my voice was too weak to be heard. I knew it then, and I know it now. So why, twenty-five years later, was I shouting at Salim, You're not in bed yet? Where have you been? Are you such a grown man, then, that you can go against me and stay out all night?

He had gotten home at 2 am. As far as I could see, he was drunk. I had more to say, more to shout into his face, but I didn't recognise the voice that was coming from me.

It wasn't my voice. My father's voice, in the black fortress of the entryway to his home, bruised my face and head. The next morning I was adjusting my turban as I got ready to leave when Salim came into my room. He still looked drunk and he said to me, Dad, I'm really sorry, really I am. And then he went out.

When I said to Mayya, furiously, and not for the first time, I told you, this son of yours is good for nothing, she made excuses for him. His exams were just over, she said, and all of his classmates were out on the town. He was not a boy any more.

Viper

Zarifa rapped hard on the door. Sanjar! Get out here, boy.

He was there immediately. Mama! Everything all right?

She would not come into his room. They walked through the broad front courtyard of the Big House and out to the little alleyways that were palely lit by the wan flows of light coming from the houses on either side.

Is it true what I heard, Sanjar? Is it true, you'd leave your own home town, your family too, you'd go away?

Yes, it's true, he said. Come with me if you want to.

She pounced on him, her arms so hard around his neck that she practically throttled him. You give your little girl this strange name, *Rasha*, which no one around here would ever name her daughter, and you want to leave town too?

He shook off her grip roughly. His voice was loud now. Listen, Mama! I don't care what my daughter's name is – yes, if she'd been a boy I'd have named her Muhammad or Hilal or Abdallah—

What? Zarifa shouted. Merchant Sulayman would kill you! You'd give your child a name he gave one of his children? Are you crazy, boy? Who do you think you are? And who raised you in his own home and gave you an education and got you married?

He spoke through clenched teeth. Listen to me. Merchant Sulayman raised me and, yes, he put me through a little schooling, and he found me a wife, but it was all for his own self-interest, all because he meant me to serve him, and to have my wife as his servant too, and then my children later on. No, Zarifa, no! Merchant Sulayman has no claim on me. We are free – the law says so, free, Zarifa. Open your eyes. The world has changed but you just keep on saying the same words over and over: *ya hababi, ya sidi*, my master, my honoured master. While everybody's gotten educated and gotten jobs, you've stayed exactly where you always were, the slave of Merchant Sulayman like that is all there is. He's just an old man who can't even keep his hands steady! Open your eyes, Zarifa. We are free, and everyone is his own master, and no one owns anyone else. I am free and I can travel wherever and whenever I like and I can name my children whatever I want to name them. If it's what you want, then stay with him, the old fool. Fine. Just stay then.

Zarifa was on the point of slapping him, an automatic response left over from all those years of devilish boyhood – years which weren't so far behind them, after all. Too quick for her, he stepped back and with her hand missing him, she lost her balance, teetered and fell, colliding with the base of the wall.

A woman from the village happened to be in the same alleyway. Hearing Zarifa's sobs, she ran over. Like a woman in mourning, Zarifa threw her arms up and clapped them around her shoulders. Their heads together, shaking, they sobbed. The boy's gone, the boy's gone and left me, he talks just like his father. He's making no sense, like his papa, and he's going away like him too. Free, free! That's what he always says. His father tormented me with such talk. I couldn't believe it when Habib left and now his son here sounds just like him. Free, not slaves! What does any of this matter to me? I want my son here with me. That viper woman of his puts ideas in his head, she tells him to leave me and go away, she wants my heart to burn to ashes. And where's he to go? What'll he work at? Who will feed him and keep him safe? My son, my boy, my only one, he's gone, gone…

The other woman, her arms around Zarifa, was sobbing just as hard.

But it wasn't Sanjar's wife, Shanna, who'd had the idea, even if she was ready enough to encourage it.

Soon after Shanna's father, Zayd, had died, the year before, Zarifa announced to the young woman that she would betroth her to Sanjar. Shanna had been delirious with joy. Getting married meant getting out of her collapsing house and away from her family, and that was the most she could hope for. Marrying any man on the face of the earth would do that. Sanjar had nothing, of course, but she'd learned that he was hoping to go away sooner or later, leaving this entire country behind. She was bored with al-Awafi – its people, its animals, the mountains and farms – and she shared Sanjar's fierce yearning for a new life in a place far away where there weren't any poor people, or where at least, maybe, they could climb out of the poverty that dogged them here. She was fed up with being poor, with the filth and the begging that went along with having nothing. She was tired of a life that held no touch of style or refinement, or – and this was likely worse – a life in which she was always able to see nice things but never to have them. She was tired of carrying water on her head every morning and evening, of the smoke from their cooking fires and the dust cloud she stirred up whenever she had to sweep the house. But what really disgusted her, more than al-Awafi and its people and animals and poverty and service, was her mother Masouda.

Ever since Shanna had opened her eyes on life, this mother of hers had been a bent and twisted creature – a crooked form whose lashless eyes were swollen and whose hands were ever dry and cracked. When Shanna got older, she would hear that her mother's permanently bowed back was the result of constantly stooping over the short-handled broom she'd always used to sweep the courtyard, and of course from carrying heavy loads of firewood day after day.

Shanna avoided Masouda as much as she possibly could and showed her aversion as thoroughly as a girl could do without stirring up too many comments or rumours. And as if this ill-starred mother's misery weren't enough, her husband's death had left her in a peculiar condition. She's gone out of her mind, of course, Shanna muttered to herself repeatedly, just as she said to everyone else. She could not understand how her father could have felt anything at all for this woman who had spent her entire life carrying wood and sweeping the floor. It had always astonished Shanna to find the two of them spending the long evenings talking, even laughing together sometimes. Her father was a strong man – why, he was known as the fellow who could hoist two huge sacks of rice or two enormous bags of dates without any show of stress. For her mother, he had built this house out of gypsum with his own hands. He'd had the means to marry another woman but he didn't. He stuck with this strange wife of his, seemingly fond of her and her odd ways. Many times, Shanna had said to herself, If he had married someone else then maybe now she, Shanna, would have brothers and sisters who could share some of the irritating burden of this mother. But as Zarifa – soon to become her mother-in-law – would always say, The beast of burden is made for burdens.

How could she know what might have happened, anyway? Likely those imaginary brothers and sisters would have washed their hands of her mother, because she was only their father's elder wife, and they would have left Shanna with all the misery and toil of taking care of her. In any case

Sanjar would emigrate as his father had done before him and then Shanna would be rid of the worry and the drudgery. She would no longer have to hear this monotonous tinny insistent voice that made the base of her skull vibrate. I'm over here! It's Masouda. I'm Masouda and I'm here. Always that voice, embarrassing Shanna in front of the neighbours and shaming her before all the people of al-Awafi.

She hated them. She hated them all.

Abdallah

No sooner did Muhammad free himself of his obsessive attachment to the whirling fan than he became engrossed in another game: opening and shutting the door. He spent all of his waking hours yanking it open and then banging it shut, over and over, with never a pause. We tried desperately to interest him in some other activity, anything, or to get him to repeat the few unconnected words he could pronounce. All was in vain.

When I left the house, Muhammad would always insist that his mother stay immediately next to him as he opened and closed the door. She did not say a word. When I'd had enough of the company of my friends and the cafés we sat in, I would return home to find the two of them exactly as I had left them. Muhammad would be repeating his random words like a parrot, his mother there at his side. Eventually, out of sheer exhaustion he would collapse and fall sleep. She would go to sleep immediately, waking up only when he did.

One day I came back when Mayya was taking a bath. The sound of the door opening and shutting, opening and shutting, opening and shutting, began to erode my sanity, and it was all I could do to keep from knocking Muhammad's head against that door of his or cuffing him. I wished he would open the window instead of the door, perch there for a moment, and fly right through it. Yes, I wanted Muhammad to fly out the window like the birds and never come back, if only that would stop this unending, never-changing sound for good.

Salima

Azzan informed Salima that he had accepted the request made by Khalid, son of Emigrant Issa, for the hand of his daughter Asma, and that he had excused himself to the Emigrant's family for not accepting Khalid's brother for Khawla, telling them that she had already been reserved for her cousin.

Salima flashed him an angry look. Her cousin who? she snapped. Nasir, that boy we haven't heard a peep from in more than four years? Who never has asked after us or her? Since when is Khawla reserved? What is this talk? Where is he, this cousin of hers? Out on the streets like a tramp, miserable fellow, somewhere in Canada – and we refuse someone who really wants to marry our girl?

Azzan turned his face away. I have responded to them and there is nothing more to say. If you want to make preparations for your daughter Asma's wedding and agree with the women in Khalid's family about the dowry and the arrangements, then go ahead. But Khawla – no.

He threw a wool shawl over his shoulders and went out as he did every night.

Salima walked quietly into the middle room. Mayya was asleep. She picked up the baby, undid her swaddling and began rubbing oil and salt into her reddened navel. The tiny girl opened her eyes and stared at Salima. The baby's grandmother could not keep back a tear or two as she remembered Muhammad, who had died as a nursing baby. She was trying not to remember Hamad – Hamad whom this baby so resembled, the son she had lost. She didn't want to remember him at all.

She wrapped the baby up again tightly and settled the little bundle on her lap. She examined her face for a moment and closed her eyes. Opening them, it was not her granddaughter that she saw. She didn't even see Muhammad or Hamad, her two dear departed ones, nor did she see Azzan's glum face. Her eyes weren't taking in the blue paint on the walls or the shelves set into their thicknesses, where the porcelain sat on display. What she saw was her uncle's house.

Her uncle's house? No, what she really saw was the thin line where the high thick wall of that fortress met the sky.

How many years had plodded by as she leaned against the kitchen's outside wall, listening to the slave women quarrelling inside and the slave men's jokes and shouting on the other side, the children screaming and fighting in the courtyard, the high-pitched screech of her uncle's wife belting out commands. And no one ever listened to Salima, and no one ever spoke to her.

So many years had passed as she leaned there, against that wall, unseen and unheard, staring at the line where the wall met the sky.

Many times since those days, she had tried to remember what her feelings were as she leant there slumped against the wall. Did she feel any sadness when she learned her father had died? Did she feel any longings for her mother? Was she angry? She didn't remember any of these things, though she tried. All she recalled was a sun so bright it hurt her eyes and the odour of kitchen smoke everywhere. She did remember one sensation especially well: hunger.

People used to talk, back then, about the impact of the world war, the terrible inflation and all of the unrest among the tribes, but she did not understand what any of it had to do with the way her uncle's wife stared at her niece's hands and mouth as the family ate their main midday meal. Ever since her father's death, when her uncle had insisted on moving her and Muaadh to his home, Salima had forgot what breakfast tasted like. The adults drank coffee and ate dates but she always waited for lunchtime to come.

When they had guests from another tribe, Salima could smell the fragrance of meat grilling, and the broth and freshly baked paper-thin bread as the visiting men ate with her uncle. Then she, her uncle's children and his wife gathered around the leftovers on the enormous tray that had been prepared for the guests. Usually there wasn't anything more than a little broth and some bones with hardly any meat on them. Her uncle's children fought over the remnants of food while her uncle's wife trained her eyes on Salima's hand. Salima would feel her hand must be huge every time she reached toward the tray. Her mouth was very big and ugly, she was certain. When there weren't any guests, lunch was dried sardines that had been pounded and mixed with onion, lemon and water, along with a few dates. Rice was so expensive that only invalids were fed it. She hated the acrid smell of the dried-out sardines but since most of the time she was so hungry that her tummy ached, she ate the mixture anyway.

Yes, hunger. That was what she remembered of her life in her uncle's home.

The baby's shrill cry demanded Salima's attention. She was hungry, of course. Mayya, sang out her mother, get yourself up now, nurse your baby girl.

Mayya struggled upright and managed to nurse her baby until the infant fell asleep. She lay down again, stretching out quietly on her mat. Her mother carried in a big smooth stone, laid it over the lit coals, and a few moments later wrapped it in a towel to preserve its heat while protecting Mayya's skin from scorching. Mayya exposed her belly and her mother placed the stone there, wrapping her and the stone up together like a package in a tattered old length of fabric. Twice every day for forty days Mayya had to endure the added heat of the stone on her belly so that her middle would not collapse into flabby post-birth wrinkles. The stone did not annoy her half as much as did the tightly wrapped cloth, over her belly and around her body, night and day, for forty whole days, until she was cleansed of her afterbirth and would emerge with a sleek, taut belly.

Entering the room, Asma broke into a smile at the sight of the swaddled stone on Mayya's middle. I'll be going to buy the gold, Salima said to her. And the clothes and wedding chest, all for your wedding. Next month.

Asma nodded, smiling to herself, anticipating her own experience of motherhood. Why wasn't there even one book, among all of the volumes on her shelves, which singled out motherhood as the radiant experience it must be? Had her grandfather, Shaykh Masoud, whose library her mother had inherited, not been interested in motherhood? Or were books in general reticent on this subject? She didn't know the answer to that one, since she had never seen another library in her life.

Azzan and Qamar

Azzan's head lay in Qamar's lap, his eyes fixed on the stars glittering in the soft clear desert sky. She was gliding her fingertips along his lashes and brows and flicking off the grains of sand clinging there, putting them in her mouth. He was accustomed to this gesture of hers now, so it no longer startled him. He floated in the ecstasy of her words, captured by her intensity which never seemed to lessen, her zealous attention to house, camels, work and brother. When she suddenly went silent he rubbed his cheek against her hand. Keep talking, I love your voice. She lay down next to him in the sand. Fingers interlaced beneath their heads, together they gazed at the constellation Ursa Minor which was unmistakeable at this time of year.

You speak, whispered Qamar. You hardly ever say anything.

Azzan sighed. But a moment later he did begin speaking. He told her about a long-ago wound that was still alive. His son Hamad.

From birth, Hamad had been a weak and wan-looking baby. His mother expected him to die at any moment, as had her first baby, Muhammad, who had died before he was even two months old. She had Hamad wearing every kind of amulet that she could get a shaykh to prescribe. Azzan lost the hopes he had had for the boy.

But Hamad lived. His tiny body fought hard, resisting the fate of his brother, and he made his way in life – and what life there was in him! So constantly in motion was the boy that he could barely eat or sleep. It was almost impossible to see him still or quiet. He was always scampering around or chattering away.

Azzan began to let himself hope. This boy would be his successor. This boy would carry his father's legacy – his name and property. This was the boy on whom he would depend in his old age. Hamad's mother left his hair alone to grow long like a girl's, hoping to fool the jinn, to evade the destructive envy that might target her son. The leather and silver amulets were still there, concealed under his clothing, until he reached the age of eight and died.

He couldn't dodge fate, as his parents had always worried and silently suspected. But death took its time. Death gave their hearts time to swell, years enough to grow heavy with love for him, and only then it took him.

Qamar swallowed. What happened to him?

Azzan smiled slowly and closed his eyes. What happened to him was what happened to the Range Rover.

Range Rover? You mean, a car?

Azzan's thin smile turned to a bitter smirk. Yes, the green Range Rover.

When the fever struck Hamad down and it was no longer any use to rub herbal preparations onto his burning body, Salima walked to her uncle's house. Shaykh Said had grown old by then but he had not grown soft enough that his heart would melt at her entreaties. She pleaded with him to remember his brother Shaykh Masoud, her father. She begged him to be merciful, to think of his faith. She spoke in the name of the generosity, high mindedness and honour befitting a shaykh. Everything she could possibly think of, she said, as a mother whose child was lacerated by fever.

His response didn't change. The Range Rover doesn't leave al-Awafi unless I'm in it.

The next day Hamad's fever shot even higher. The boy was delirious. This time Azzan went with Salima to her uncle's house. Azzan talked to the shaykh for a long time, explaining that his son's condition was very bad and growing worse, and the only car in al-Awafi was Shaykh Said's Range Rover, and they needed to rush Hamad to Saada Hospital in Maskad. If they went by donkey it would take four or five days, too long to save the boy. Azzan would pay whatever Shaykh Said asked for and would cover the driver's pay as well.

Shaykh Said said, I don't have anything more to say. The Range Rover doesn't leave al-Awafi, and your son can get well without those doctors. All children get fevers and then they're fine.

Azzan and Salima left his house avoiding looking at the green vehicle hunched at the door. Shaykh Said had bought it two years before. When his driver brought it grandly into al-Awafi, absolutely everyone came out of their homes to witness it. Even Shaykh Said's ancient mother, leaning on her slave women, came out to see it. But when she heard the motor and saw its black wheels whirling, she threw a rock at it, calling out to the people of al-Awafi that it was the work of the Devil. Her rock broke one of the windows. Shaykh Said ordered her women to take his mother inside, threatening that if they ever brought her out again when the car was there, he would whip them then and there, in full daylight for all to see. From that day on, the car never budged except when Shaykh Said occupied the front passenger seat. If one of his wives was in the car he covered all the windows with curtains.

Salima cried all the way home. Now Azzan's dreams held only one image: the car he must have. He swore he would take permission to buy one from the Sultan himself, as Shaykh Said had done. He would own a car even if he had to sell his farm – his whole inheritance – to do it.

But Hamad didn't wait until his father filled his vow. The fever killed him first.

They removed his clothes and his amulets, and they erected the ritual bench made of dried date-palm fibre in the courtyard. Neighbours brought buckets of water from the canal to wash him. They sprinkled him with incense and perfumed him with aloes-wood oil, and wrapped his body in a white shroud. The funeral procession marched to the graveyard west of al-Awafi.

Judge Yusuf said to Azzan, Your son is in heaven, and he will be there to bring you cold water when you are thirsty. You know, Azzan, that your child will serve you in heaven, on the day of Judgement, as long as you are patient with God's will. Be consoled for it was God who took your son.

Azzan said nothing. He did not say to the judge that he had wanted his son to bring him cold water in his old age, still on earth. He bore himself with resignation as was expected, and shook hands with those who came to offer their condolences. He shook every hand that was outstretched to his, even Shaykh Said's.

Tears fell from the Moon's eyes. Aah, it's true what the proverb says: Every father knows misery and pain.

From Hamad's burial to this day, Azzan told her, he had never spoken about his son. Only now. She turned to him. Even with his mother? He shook his head. Especially not with his mother.

As they spoke, Salima was slipping cautiously out of a house in al-Awafi. She had just come from a very important appointment. She walked quickly, so that she would be certain to be back at home before Azzan could return from his evening with the Bedouin men.

She tried to avoid thinking about how dark it had been in there, or about the conditions set for this peculiar agreement. But the last sentence the man had said, when she was already at the door, pounded insistently in her head. Don't worry, Bride of the Falaj! Ugh, she thought. These people who never forget! Her daughter had married and given birth, and another daughter was engaged, but people still called her by this hateful nickname. Angry, she quickened her pace, wanting to be at home.

Abdallah

When Mayya had got through her forty days, I brought her home, back to our living quarters, a small wing attached to my father's house. She stayed there, secluded, closing her ears to the words that had spread through al-Awafi like fire across dry wood. People were whispering about a relationship between her father and an enticing Bedouin woman.

At that time I was driving my father's white Mercedes between Muscat and al-Awafi several times every week. I spent my long commutes musing that the peaceful happiness I enjoyed was almost too much for me. Was it too much, this feeling that I had it all? It made me nervous.

Did I deserve such happiness, or didn't I? A happy man driving his father's car to his own home, where the wife he loves holds their child, and where his father presides, still alive and even healthy.

That's what I was, a happy man. Simply that. A young man, barely past his first twenty years, whose dreams reached no further than what he had in his hands. But he was a little afraid of what he held in his hands. The dark interior of the Mercedes, the glancing light reflected in the shiny buttons on tiny London's clothes, the drops of water falling from Mayya's hair at dawn, the flash of the needle in her hand as she sewed fabric flowers onto Baby London's gowns, my father's rare smiles. In all of it I saw – me, the so-very-lucky man – that this happiness was a lot for me to bear. It was too much for me. Somehow I knew that – whatever the reason, and I had no idea what it might be – I was not worthy of all this joy.

Zarifa

Ah, Zarifa! You were wrong to believe that Habib had gone forever. No, Zarifa, it doesn't work like that. Habib was careful to plant his seeds in his son. The young shoots would grow to prick and wound you, just as Habib gave you pain.

Habib, whether you are lying cold in some faraway grave, or whether you drowned in the Shatt al-Arab, or whether you're even still alive and making money in Dubai or Baluchistan, wherever and however you may be now, if only you could have left us before you sowed the Devil's own seeds!

We are free, Mother. Free according to the law. And we will name our children whatever we like.

Your son went mad, Zarifa. No, it wasn't on account of the viper he married, that woman who was so rebellious and so disrespectful to her mother, it wasn't she who insinuated these ideas in his head. It was the seed, the one his father carefully planted before he could disappear.

Ayy, Habib! The more I wanted to forget you and the wretched trouble you made, the larger your seed grew in my eyes, grew and grew until the pressure was too great and my eyes exploded.

Merchant Sulayman – who raised him and supported him,

and put him through school – he called *the raving mad old man*.

Can't he see that we grew up by the grace of that old man? If it weren't for him, we'd be begging in the streets now or calling out to passers-by for a mouthful of rice, like pitiful Maneen does.

Free . . . we are free.

This boy Sanjar wants to disrespect you and leave, just like his wife the viper scorned her mother and left her to the charity of the neighbourhood women.

Poor, poor Masouda. Yes, she was jealous of you, Zarifa, all those days when you didn't have to go out into the desert at sunrise to gather wood as she did. All of your work was inside the house, and when you went out to draw water from the falaj, you used the outing as an opportunity to visit the women you liked in the neighbourhood. But she, poor thing, had to bend double from the burden of the wood on her back, day after day, year after year.

She was patient about all the toil and misery, and about her husband. No sooner would Zayd finish with one woman than he would go after another. What do you have to say, Zarifa? Seek God's forgiveness! The dead deserve only mercy. God have mercy on him, he was also my relative. And the proverb-maker says: Your nose is still your own even if it's putrid to the bone. God give him mercy.

Now, here's her girl Shanna, with eyes like a tiger's – but who do you blame, Zarifa? You insisted that Sanjar marry her because you worried over him. Are you at peace now? He wants to go far away, and he says to you, Come with us.

Go with you where? So, we should leave the land that's ours, the place where we live, the country of our family and our ancestors for some strange world where we don't know the people or what's what? And Merchant Sulayman – who will watch after him? Who will bake his bread? His sister whose nose is permanently in the air? What she did to poor Fatima, to that poor woman, mother of Abdallah! God give her mercy. People have no mercy in this world.

How can you leave al-Awafi, Zarifa, when you barely know any other spot in God's wide world? It's all your fault, Habib, all of it. The words you kept repeating in front of Sanjar when the boy was still in nappies.

Your wild savage laugh in the depths of the night still tears my heart apart. Your country and your ancestors' country? What ancestors, Zarifa? Your ancestors aren't from here. They were as black as you are, they were from Africa, from the lands from where they stole you, all of you, and sold you.

It's useless, Zarifa, to try telling this man that no one stole you. That you were born a slave because your mother was a slave and that's the way life is. That slavery passes to you from your mother. That no one stole you, and al-Awafi is your place, its people are yours.

Habib spat in your face whenever you said such things to him. He did not want to banish that memory, to forget the terrifying journey that ended his calm, pleasant life in Makran. The second child of his mother who had five boys in all, he remembers everything: the local gangs that attacked their village wanting money, or perhaps to pay old scores; the merchants, a jumble of Baluchs and Arabs, who bought them, there on the plains; the filthy crammed ships those merchants packed them into; the eye disease that spread fast from one child to the next on shipboard; his mother's screaming for her other children, who'd been shoved onto other boats; the nursing baby who died of smallpox while on her breast, so the slave traders snatched him away and threw him into the sea.

We are free. They stole us, and then they sold us! he would scream in the middle of the night, at dawn, in the zar exorcisms: Free! They did us wrong, they destroyed us. Free!

He and his mother were sold when they reached the east coast of Oman. The slave traders sold them to other slave traders, until finally Merchant Sulayman bought them. Habib's mother wept for years. People in al-Awafi were sympathetic when they heard her story, but no one could find out where her other children had been sent, and as for her being returned to her own land, that was out of the question. Anyway, highwaymen and pirates would simply steal her and sell her again. There was no doubt about that in anyone's mind.

Azzan and Qamar

Azzan held Najiya's face between his hands as he repeated the lines that Majnun had said to his Layla.

Light the dimness with your glow once the full moon dips
and shine in the sun's stead whilst lazy dawn tarries
Your radiance outdoes the brightest sun there be:
it can never thieve your smile, steal your pearly mouth
The resplendent night, your countenance! tho' the full moon rise
a moon bereft of your breast, of this graceful throat I see
Whence would the morning sun ever find a ready kohl-stick
to etch for its pale face these languid eyes of yours?
What starry siren can mime coy Layla when her form spirals away
or her eyes, the winsome startled pools of the sands' wild mare?

Najiya laughed quizzically. The sands' wild mares?

Azzan stroked her face. This is the most beautiful sort of animal, Qamar, and Layla's Crazed Lover tells you for certain, Qamar, my Moon, that your beauty is a gift from the Creator. That from you streams more light than the sun and moon together can ever give, and that your eyes are more beautiful than the eyes of the wild desert mare.

Her beauty was so strong it hurt him; her sharp glow splintered his chest with a murky roiling pain. All he could do then was to recite poetry to her. Before she knew him, names like al-Mutanabbi, Ibn al-Rumi, al-Buhturi, and Majnun Layla – Layla's Crazed Lover – were just pale ghosts from books, lifeless figures that belonged to the hated world of school and the boring books full of words they'd had to memorise. Azzan made these dead images breathe. Najiya began to feel al-Mutanabbi's insomnia, his ambitions and his frustrations, as if they were her own. She imagined al-Buhturi sitting on the right hand of the Caliph Mutawakkil, the two of them gazing out across the lake that al-Buhturi immortalised in his poetry. The image of Imru'l-Qays pursued by the night that lowered its curtains over him like the waves of the sea dazzled her. Now, she would end her long evening chats with Azzan by chanting Imru'l-Qays's words – al-yawmu khamrun wa-ghadan amrun – Wine we'll drink today, tomorrow's command they'll bray – to remind him of the heavy tasks that were waiting for her the next day. Though she felt some sympathy for al-Maarri in his blindness, she didn't understand his poems nor did she like his insistence that the surface of the earth is made of nothing but the remnants of bodies. Najiya was all for life. She was passionate about it, and poetic lines that celebrated love and the tribal zeal of old delighted her. She could not warm up to poems of quiet contemplation, a puritan withdrawal from life, or the Sufi mystical way.

It didn't help that Azzan would sink into a state of gloom at the very thought of the late Judge Yusuf with whom he had learned this poetry and the Sufi way of spiritual passion that sat so uneasily now, for him, with his cravings for Najiya. One day she witnessed Azzan slide into an unfathomable grief after he began repeating the lines by Shaykh Said, son of Khalfan al-Khalili, who had been, he told her, an important scholar and political leader of their region in the nineteenth century, the right-hand man of the Imam Azzan, son of Qays, and at the same time a man of steely will who could renounce worldly things.

Neither exertion nor acceptance can I claim to possess
only a mere affinity in which I find my pride
Nor have I strength to wish myself into their clutches
how can my wished-for goal be theirs and not be wrong?
My purpose is to see no willed-for purpose there
the essence of will this is, the wish-eye of the blind.

As time went on, Najiya began reacting to Azzan's nervous poetic intensity by recoiling from any mention of poetry, Or at least she tried to place limits on it in her own mind, by reducing anything smacking of poetry to her own fancies about these poets who had loved life, or who had gone over the edge as a result of meeting beautiful women, among whom she saw herself, of course, and especially Layla, beloved of al-Majnun, the Crazed.

Abdallah

My aunt is enormously tall. When I was little I used to think of her as a skeletal minaret soaring over a mosque and casting a threadlike shadow. Something about the fact that she was taller than Zarifa aggravated me, though she couldn't compete with Zarifa in overall bulk. That, at least, made me feel a bit better. Zarifa's bosom was splendidly ample for a little boy to snuggle into and sleep. When she hugged me her hands and arms practically buried me alive. My aunt, on the other hand, had no chest to speak of. Gold rings brightened her thin white hand. Both wrists were swaddled in a dozen heavy, intricately-worked bracelets that made their own distinct clanging whenever she lifted an arm to point her thin fingers aggressively at someone. I couldn't imagine her hands engaged in any activity, except for poking their skinny fingers imperiously into the faces of others.

I did not understand the secret behind her never-ending presence in my father's house even though she had been married to a maternal cousin of hers who lived in another town. She was scornful of everyone and treated them with an eccentric, exaggerated etiquette that belittled them mercilessly. She didn't have much to say. When the neighbourhood women came by, out of politeness, when she was in our house, she would barely touch their hands in greeting, quickly and ostentatiously pulling back her own heavily hennaed fingertips, inviting them to sit down as she made a clear sign to Zarifa to bring the coffee in quickly. They would sit down and exchange hasty, abrupt words, almost cutting each other off, as if the fact of her severe presence prevented them from holding more drawn-out or relaxed conversations. As soon as they finished their dates and coffee my aunt would shift in her seat and they would get up to leave immediately as if shrugging the duty of the visit off their shoulders. There was an unspoken understanding that they were absolutely not to bring their children. My aunt despised children more than she did anything or anyone else.

The sharp crevices in my aunt's face contrasted with Zarifa's broad, flat face. She was the only one who treated Zarifa like any other slave and would never acknowledge her status – which everyone recognised even if no one ever said anything – as the person in charge of my father's household, not to mention his long-time mistress. My aunt was determined, even throughout the long stretches when my father was very ill, to sit right outside his room, opposite the doorway, just so that her presence would prevent Zarifa from ever slipping in to see him.

She and my father practised an elaborate ritual of mutual respect that was acutely embarrassing in its obvious artificiality. But for these long strings of greetings they exchanged, which followed exactly the same pattern every time, they never said a word to each other. Only when I was much older did I understand the extent to which their demonstrations of respect carried a profound contempt that extended to hatred. If she was directing a silent war against Zarifa, my father's presence and the fact of their relationship enabled Zarifa to show her enmity toward my aunt in front of us: we little ones, all of the slaves, and indeed everyone in al-Awafi. Zarifa usually focused her disparagements of my aunt on her lack of luck with men: she had been divorced twice, by two brothers and, Zarifa said, that dry, sticklike body of hers was barren.

But Zarifa could not completely conceal her fear of my aunt. Perhaps that's why, soon after my father died, she left the Big House and went to join her son in Kuwait.

Asma

After a three-day shopping trip to Muscat with her prospective son-in-law and his mother, Salima returned to al-Awafi loaded down with Asma's wedding things, which she had gotten from the shops in Matrah where you could find every conceivable wedding item. But, she confided to Muezzin-Wife, she wasn't overjoyed with her purchases. There's nicer things out there, she said, and Asma deserves them. But her father – may God ease his path – refused to set a dowry payment for the bridegroom.

Is my daughter a piece of merchandise to be sold? That's what he snapped at me when I asked. Her dowry will be the same as anyone else's, he said to me. So her fiancé only paid two thousand riyals, since he wasn't asked to come up with any more than that. His mama was silent the whole time. It seems that she's been away from her home town too long to remember how we do things here.

Still, Salima spread out the purchases for display, as they watched: Asma, Khawla, the muezzin's wife, Judge Yusuf's widow, Umm Nasir and three more women who lived nearby. Their outstretched hands competed to turn over and examine the shimmering silk fabric that Mayya would make into dishdashas and sirwals, all heavily embroidered, for the bride.

Salima brought out the translucent head wrappings, green cloth embroidered along the edges in gold flowers, and others with sequins sewn into their borders.

Though she did her best to resist, at least for a few minutes, Khawla had to reach for the shiny pair of high-heeled sandals: Salima levelled a warning glance at her as she tried them on. Once everyone had had her say about the fabrics, Salima opened the perfume chest: two bottles of French perfume that Salima had bought because the mother of the groom insisted, though she would have preferred to put the money into a third vial of pure oud perfume.

Muezzin-Wife laughed. Salima, oud has turned your senses! Surely one bottle is enough for this bride.

Salima answered earnestly. How can you have a bride without plenty of oud? Look at the incense, I bought two kinds for her: real, pure Cambodian aloes-wood oil and the best incense, from Salalah. Khawla, heat up some coals and we'll try it out.

Khawla jumped up and hurried toward the kitchen. Asma was muttering. Mama, incense chokes me. I wish you had bought me more perfume instead.

Quiet, you don't understand anything, Salima said, bringing out the chest that held the gold. Did you ever hear of a bride getting married without incense? What an awful scandal that would be!

The women's shining eyes replicated and doubled the gold's lustre as they inspected it: a heavy link necklace, one with several thin strands, rings bearing a variety of stones, and a diamond ring, a gift from the groom's mother. There were also thin bangles and one broad and heavy spiked bracelet.

In our days the jewellery was silver, remarked one of the neighbours. Praise God – how times have changed.

True, said another, it was silver, but at least we had anklets, enough to announce that one of us was coming with the ringing they made against each other, and the bracelets we wore high up on our arms. And the hair ornaments, too.

Salima was clearly irritated. You know girls these days, they don't like wearing anklets or our heavy armlets.

Of course not, said Asma. I don't want to wear things that are going to scratch up my legs and feet.

She picked up her new jewellery, examining it with some curiosity. When she saw the gold bangle with the spikes she started giggling. She couldn't help remembering the story of Judge Yusuf's wife with an old-fashioned bracelet like this. At the time, bracelets were indeed silver or they might be plated thinly with gold. Maryam, Judge Yusuf's widow, had told Asma the story herself.

WAllahi, my dear, I wasn't more than fourteen. My mother – God be merciful to her – came to me and said, Come on, Maryam, now praise your Lord and put on these new clothes of yours, and your new bracelets and silver amulets.

Why, Mama?

You are getting married to Judge Yusuf today.

I cried so hard my eyes swelled up, but no one paid any attention to me. In the evening all the women of the neighbourhood swarmed in. They were singing and they picked me up and carried me to the judge, a whole procession of them. At the door my mother broke eggs over my feet and whispered to me: Listen, Maryam, watch out you don't let that man find you too ready, like a ripe watermelon about to split open. You defend yourself, now, so we can hold our heads high. You just go at him with these bracelets on your wrist. Yes, hit him, that's right, don't be a juicy watermelon just waiting there for him.

By God, my girl! Asma, I went for a whole month pounding him every night with those bracelets, bruising him up like my mother told me to do. He would say to me, Maryam,

Maryuuuma dear, my Maryuumii, what do you want me to call you? Just tell me!

I wouldn't take those bracelets off my wrist for anything. I swung them right in front of his nose whenever he came near. God give you mercy, Abu Abd al-Rahman! What a man of learning he was! He read all the books of religion and knowledge and understanding, and he tried so hard to sweeten me up, the poor fellow! Maryuuma, he would say, I just want to talk to you. Why are you attacking me? Listen to me, talk to me! There's no reason to scream at me, and to scratch me, every day and the next. If you hate me that much I'm not going to force myself on you. It would not be right for me to force you. Did your family force you to marry me, Maryam? Do you hate me, Maryuuma?

Wallahi, my girl, Asma, I didn't hate him at all, he was a lot better than my father or my brothers or anyone else. He was the protector of knowledge and faith, God grant him His lenience and make his grave as spacious as he made my world! My dear, I was just listening to my mama, only doing what she said to do. Trying not to be a soft watermelon.

Asma was laughing. And so – what happened after a month, Umm Abd al-Rahman?

Maryam smiled and waved the question away. Ahh, a month later, my girl, my Asma – what was written by the hand of fate happened. I told you he was careful to be understanding and gentle, and I was just a young girl, and the world has to move ahead. They were written for us, these seeds that made my belly swell. Abd al-Rahman and his brothers and sisters, God be merciful to their father, he was always patient with me, when every two or three days I'd get angry with him and go off to my family without any cause for it. He would say to me: You're my wife, Maryuuma, in this world and the next, and you are as dear to me as Aisha, God be pleased with her, was dear to the Prophet, God's prayers and blessings upon him. The judge died so young, my poor dear fellow. The good folks don't stay with us long, Asma my dear, they leave us so quickly. But people just wouldn't keep their mouths shut. You are young, Maryam, they would say. Marry again, the living stay with us longer than the dead. Allah! No, just imagine – marry again, after Judge Abu Abd al-Rahman? How could I do such a thing, since he used to say to me, You are my wife in this world and the next, Maryuuma. In this world and in the next.

Khawla came out with the lit coals. Salima sprinkled incense over them and held the mixture in front of the neighbours, each in turn. They began teasing each other, since if the smoke of the incense could be seen rising from their garments, that meant Salima was truly fond of them, but if it got caught there and didn't rise, it meant she didn't like them much. As she made her rounds they started exclaiming, Heh! Look, the incense is coming out of the sleeves of Muezzin-Wife but no one else's. We don't get a share in what's fair!

Salima was occupied now in unrolling the hand-worked cushion covers for them to see, and measuring the lengths of the two carpets she had bought after a long quarrel with the Iranian shop owner. Khawla leaned toward Asma and whispered, A bride's trousseau but no nightgowns or make-up – my poor sister! Asma winked at her. There'll be some way to get them before the wedding, I know it.

Salima described the mandus she had ordered to her specifications from the leading producer of wood wedding chests, whose manduses were more elaborate than any others around: the precise size she wanted, exactly what kinds of work she wanted on the wood and the brass fittings, and the shape of the brass handles. Khawla interrupted her. But houses these days have bedrooms, already with a bed and wardrobe and dressing table. At that, Muezzin-Wife exclaimed, Ask God's forgiveness for what you just said! My goodness, nothing pleases girls these days – my girl, a bride without a mandus isn't a bride. After all, that mandus of hers will keep her incense fresh for years.

Before the neighbourly gathering broke up Salima gave each of them a head wrap from the hundred she had bought to hand out to the women of al-Awafi: neighbours, the poor, relatives and others who weren't related to her, mistresses of the town's households and the women of slave families.

Abdallah

Seconds after I hit Salim I was assailed by a terrible and overwhelming sense that I had just become my father's twin. Two days later, Mayya made a point of mentioning that Salim had not been drunk at all. He had had a shock, while spending the evening – most of the night, really – with his friends in a café in upscale al-Qurm, where the music was probably very loud. Late in the evening, the patrons had dwindled. Sitting on his own, drinking lemonade with mint, he suddenly saw a hand landing on the table edge, pressing against it for support. It was impossible to ignore: the fingernails were painted a glittery silver. When Salim raised his head a young man was staring at him, as much as one could stare through half-closed eyes. He was dressed entirely in black – Versace shirt, Armani jeans – and now that Salim was looking at him, he spoke, his murmur more like a purr.

One look, man, just one, slay me.

Salim concentrated on the lemonade in his hands, but he couldn't stop himself shivering when the youth bent closer over him, tossing a fancy card onto the table. A number but no name. Salim ignored him. Where had his friends disappeared to? Maybe they were somewhere at another table, playing cards?

The young man didn't leave. He stood nearby, sighing loudly. When Salim didn't react, he made a show of putting the card down again on the table. Finally Salim had to speak.

Go – go away off now. Right now.

The youth whispered back. I know ... I don't deserve even the nails on your toes, I know that ... I don't deserve a glance ... He leaned closer in to Salim. *Allah Allah ya habibi*, the fire inside me, it's white hot, have some mercy.

When Salim hurried to his car and shot away, the boy's Porsche was right behind him, through the night-time streets of Muscat. Salim finally lost him in a side street and drove home. The clock said 2 am, and I was waiting for him in the sitting room. I hit him, my voice taut with anger. Out so late, are you? Just waiting to disobey me? Your father's rules?

Ankabuta

On the 25th of September 1926, Ankabuta was roaming the sparse expanse outside of town, bending over to pick up the few branches she could find, when the first pangs came. As she saw to the birth of her own daughter, with a rusty knife to separate the baby's life from her own, the men gathered in Geneva signed an accord. Their signatures abolished slavery and criminalised the slave trade. It was Ankabuta's fifteenth birthday but she was as unaware of that as she was that the world held a place called Geneva.

Ankabuta ripped her dusty head veil in half to make a wrapping for her newborn baby, and she stuffed the other half up herself to stop the blood. Barefoot, her face uncovered, she walked back to al-Awafi. At Shaykh Said's house – which with the birth had just gained another slave-girl – the women helped her inside. Ankabuta lay down on the reed matting and witnessed her daughter's date-feeding ritual. The women had crushed a date and put it gently in the newborn's mouth, taking it out seconds later, just as women of the Prophet's time, they'd always heard, had done. When they lay the baby down beside her, Ankabuta burst into tears at the sight of the tiny wrinkled body wrapped in half her head scarf. It was the only cloth she owned that hadn't been ripped apart by the wood she had to gather. Yes, it was only a white one – not dyed indigo like her other one, which was nearly in shreds – but it was strongly woven and held its shape. If it hadn't turned the colour of dust she would have said it was new, and now here she had lost it.

A week later the shaykh announced that the newborn girl's name was Zarifa. Unfortunately, because things had been so bad since the spoilage of the date harvest, he would not be in a position to slaughter a ritual animal. Sixteen years later he would sell the girl to Merchant Sulayman. She would become a slave worker and a concubine. She would be his beloved, and the only woman who was ever close to him, while he was the only man she would love and respect, and that until the day of her death. In him she saw her liberator from the insults of Shaykh Said's sons, and the beloved who showed her the pleasures of the body, as the instigator of the game of harshness and jealousy. In the end, he was the elderly shaykh who returned to her embrace to die.

Abdallah

At first Zayid was coming back to al-Awafi every Friday, handing out fruit, even to his neighbours. He hardly ever took off his uniform, even when he was with Suwayd, listening to him play his oud. But when no one poured coffee for him at the wake after Zayd died, leaving him to pour it himself, he knew that the villagers would never see him as a real officer. In their eyes he would always be Zayid, the son of Maneen, the wretch who begged from folks. Al-Awafi's people were firm believers in the past; they did not look to the future. Gradually Zayid stopped engaging in the life of the village. After he found an Indian maidservant for his father, his visits dwindled, until he was only making the obligatory appearances on the major holy feast days.

Years after his father's murder we heard suddenly that Zayid had got married. He did not come back to al-Awafi for the occasion. His bride – Hafiza's second and prettiest daughter – became his wife with a celebration at the Muscat Sheraton. The wedding party he arranged there was not attended by anyone from their village except the bride, her two sisters and her mother.

Hafiza couldn't have been more than seventeen when she got pregnant for the first time. Her mother Saada seized her by her hair and started pummelling her, but the neighbour women winked and let Saada know what the word was in the neighbourhood. No surprises here, Saada, she's cut from the same cloth! Before her, it was her father's sister, the slut was always lolling in the streets, wasn't she? So her mother left her alone. When the baby girl slipped out of her mama's body, her skin several shades darker than her mother's or grandmother's, Saada asked Hafiza again. Who is this bastard's father? Hafiza answered as she had before. I told you, Mama, if it wasn't Zaatar then it was either Marhun or Habib. Her mother shook her head and left her to her own devices.

When Hafiza emerged from her forty days of confinement Judge Yusuf sentenced her to a hundred lashes. Her mother stuffed a big canvas sack with whatever old rags and shirts she could find and tied it onto Hafiza's back hoping she wouldn't feel the lashes. I snuck in along with the other boys – we hid among the crowds that had collected to watch the punishment carried out. But not even two years later, Hafiza delivered her second daughter. This time, the baby had very pale skin. And the sentence changed. By then, Judge Yusuf was a magistrate under the jurisdiction of the Sultan, though earlier he had regarded himself as issuing his judgements under the last Imam Ghalib bin Ali's authority, even after the Imam was defeated and had to leave Oman. The Sultan's government did not prescribe the Sharia punishments for adultery, and so Judge Yusuf did not order the woman whipped. Some of the elders proposed that Hafiza be sent to prison but no one paid much attention any more. People whispered that the newborn looked a lot like Shaykh Said's youngest son: she was his spitting image, in fact, they said. Yet again, though, Hafiza said she wasn't certain who the father was. That's when she got her nickname, Bas ish-Shaab, Everyone's Bus. Three more years and her third daughter appeared. This one looked more or less like her own mother, and she was the last of the daughters. Soon after, someone steered Hafiza to birth control pills.

Did I doze off? Why am I so thirsty? Zarifa used to warn me about going to sleep thirsty. The sleeper who's parched, she would always say, finds his soul has left him to search, looking for something to quench his thirst. I always drank two or three glasses of water before going to bed, afraid that my soul would leave me and never return, like the man who fell asleep thirsty and his soul left him to drink from a big water jar. While it was in there drinking the lid was clamped over this soul of his. It couldn't go back to him. As they were getting ready to bury him the next morning, someone lifted the lid to get a drink himself, and the man's soul came rushing back to him.

After I stole my father's rifle for the magpies that I never tasted, my father hung me upside down and tied up in the well, to punish me, and I did go to sleep even though I was very thirsty. Many nightmares later, Masouda finally relented and told me about my mother.

Abdallah, my boy, the proverb-maker says: Daytime's for people but night-time's for the jinn. Your mama, God rest her soul in paradise, was out walking at night. She just flung away a pebble that got in her sandal perhaps. She didn't know it, but she'd hit the jinni-woman's son in the head. That jinni-woman was the servant of the Shaykhs of the Jinn. She came to your mama and she said, Pull up the basil bush in the courtyard, its smell draws vipers, and soon your son will get old enough to play there and he'll be bitten. Your mama, God take her soul to paradise, thought the jinni-woman was a poor and ordinary woman and she believed her. So at dawn she cut down the basil bush, which angered the Shaykh of the Jinn who lived beneath it. He made the poor woman sick. Two or three days, no more, and she was dead, may God keep her soul in Paradise.

When I got older, and when Shanna tried to tempt me out on the farm and I said no, she pulled her clothes together around herself and screamed, Your mama isn't dead, she's alive! They bewitched her and then they took her away. They put a plank of wood where she'd been lying down, and your papa buried it, and so your mother lost her mind. The wizard took her mind away and made her his servant. My father saw her once at night, outside town. She was all in white.

Salima

When Salima had finished arranging her daughter Asma's wedding things she closed the door to the world outside and broke down in sobs. She felt a sudden longing for her father and mother.

Salima had given birth to Khawla, the youngest of her girls, just as her own mother was giving up her soul. Really, though, her mother had died a long time before, ten years at least, when a messenger appeared to inform her that her only son, Muaadh, had died as a martyr in the war of Jabal Akhdar. She hadn't been given a chance to say her goodbyes.

When Muaadh fled the home of his uncle Shaykh Said, before the end of his sixteenth year, his uncle was furious. So, then, his hunches about the boy had proven true! He'd known that boy would split the rod of obedience to join the tribes allied with the Imam, thumbing his nose at his uncle's alliance with the opposing tribes.

Whenever people were gathered, Shaykh Said made certain to proclaim loudly that he bore no responsibility for his brother's son. He had no guilt. Does that idiot believe taking shelter in al-Jabal al-Akhdar with the Imam and his group will save him, or any of them, from the warplanes of the English? he repeated in front of anyone with ears to hear him. Those English have planes and weapons. What do *they* have, in the Green Mountain?

The Sib Treaty, signed in 1920, divided Oman into an interior ruled as an Imamate and a Government of Muscat that retained its traditional jurisdiction over much of the coastal plains. Muscat's Sultan was financed by the English. The Treaty was respected for quite a long time. But then the Sultan signed an agreement with a British firm for exploratory oil drilling in the Fahud desert, which was well within the Imamate's territories. The company formed its own defence unit, which came to be known as the Muscat-Oman Infantry. And so imperialist greed lit the wick of war, when the company army marched into Ibri and soon began strafing territories loyal to the Imami state, in the regions of Nazwa and Nakhal. In 1955 the Imam Ghalib al-Hana'i and his followers – warriors drawn from allied tribes – were forced to take refuge in the Green Mountain.

That's when Muaadh slipped out of al-Awafi and joined the fighters in the Jabal. He stayed there through 1959, one of a band of guerrilla fighters harassing the Royal British Air Force defences. The resistance had only their traditional weapons, but at least they could keep others out of the Jabal. Muaadh was tasked with lighting fires in deserted areas to convince the English that there were fighters there; the idea was that they would use up their ammunition mounting attacks against phantom platoons. One night Muaadh stepped on a small mine as he was returning from a mission. He exploded into fragments, one of more than two thousand martyrs who died in the war to control the Jabal. There wasn't even a body to return for his mother to mourn over.

She received the news of his death in silent submission. She arranged the funeral rites as well as she could in her modest circumstances, for his uncle refused to offer the slightest help or to mourn. She died, though no one knew she was dead.

Every day and every night, for ten years, she died a little more. She breathed and ate and drank but she was dead. She spoke to people and walked among them, dead. Only much later did her body give up its already-deceased spirit, its dead spirit, no longer forced to pretend, to play at being alive.

Abdallah

My head is under water. This headache lays into me every time I have to fly. I feel confused and unable to focus, and everything in front of me appears to be submerged in water. Then I sense myself being flipped upside down. I'm in a well, head down, and that heavy palm-fibre rope is wound around my body. My skull crashes against the murky black interior wall. I'm terrified that the rope will unravel, will weaken, will break and drop me to the very bottom. Why did I steal the gun? Why did I want the magpies so badly?

From my underwater head pour the many-coloured plastic blocks that Muhammad plays with. He has to have them lined up, no gaps. If there is any alteration to the way they are arranged, even one block, he screams and screams, no pauses. Screaming, Muhammad screaming.

When Uncle Ishaq's wife went into the bathroom of their home in Wadi Aday to wash before the dawn prayers she found her son in there. Pure Marwan's veins were cut open with his father's dagger. She screamed and screamed.

When my father gave up his soul in the Nahda Hospital, Zarifa screamed and the sound went on and on. I didn't scream then, I didn't cry. Only when he hung me head down in the well.

I can see myself as a little child. A boy but like a little man in disguise, wearing a man's dagger and a perfectly fitted turban, and brand-new shoes. My father's hand leads me somewhere far away. To Ibri. We are responding to the invitation of a shaykh there. Habib was with us – it was before he fled, of course – and so was Suwayd and the Bedouin who owned the two camels we rode. Suwayd's oud was not with us, though; perhaps it hadn't yet come to him. It must have been before the jinni woman fell for him, offering to answer one single wish. The oud. The bewitching oud whose sad tunes rubbed across my childhood and scored the raw loneliness of my adolescence. The oud was the gift of the jinni woman, and so Suwayd couldn't play any other instrument, only that one, solitary lute. No, there was no oud with us on that trip. There was a cloth bundle holding dried shark flesh that people ate on journeys, and some onions, and a box of dates. There was a waterskin, a lot of sand, and singing. Habib was singing, in an unfamiliar language, Baluchi maybe? It was cheerless singing and his voice would choke, coming out in a wail, when he reached some refrains. It sounded more like crying than singing. Before he fled, Habib told Zarifa that songs were the only thing left in his memory to keep his language alive for him. That's why he sang. If he didn't have songs in there, all the hollow spaces would be filled with rage.

There I was, a young fellow disguised in the uniform of his elders, the sole representative of my father's seed, paraded for the benefit of the Shaykhs of Ibri. In the souq, though, I could hardly resist reverting to my childhood state, faced with the heaps of sweet coconut spread across the stone benches to dry, and well within my reach. But I had to return to the awful dignity of my early manhood the next day, at the big midday meal with these men. I tried to sit exactly the way old men sit in the majlis meeting place, my weight on one leg while I folded the other leg beneath me, watchful, knowing

I mustn't change my position no matter how numb my legs would go, because I had to show the hardness of men. I did extend my hands to the enormous platter of rice around which we sat, but I felt so shy that my fingers could hardly grasp anything, bringing only a few grains of rice all the way back to my mouth. Some tiny bites later I finally summoned enough boldness to reach the meat piled up over the rice, securing a tiny morsel. I tried to make certain my father saw it. When the platter was lifted away I was hungry but happy, certain that my father would be satisfied with me. He had cautioned me earlier: the Shaykh's family, neighbours and slaves would be waiting expectantly for their share, whatever remained of the same platter of food that had been offered to us.

My head wasn't hanging upside down, then, and it wasn't submerged in water. My brain and heart weren't searching desperately for a sliver of land somewhere, anywhere from Muscat to Sib, where I could build the house of my wife's dreams. We couldn't manage to get the lot she really liked. The municipal authorities refused, claiming that exactly this bit of land was slated for future use: it fell within the area designated for a new rapid-transit light rail system. The planning document had already been signed off at the highest level, by the Sultan's Cabinet itself.

My head is splitting now, and the cabin pressure will certainly detonate it, until it explodes wide open. Why do I never carry headache remedies with me, like all the rest of God's travelling creatures do?

In the Shaykh's house, my hand touched the meat only after having a dozen or so little bites that were only rice, to soar in the stratosphere of my father's approval. We were nearly home when a desert viper lunged at me. If my father hadn't immediately borne down on it with his cane, killing it then and there, it would have bitten me to death. When my papa hugged me so intensely it hurt, my eyes were open to their widest and, my nose crushed against him, I breathed in the particular smell of his dishdasha. I could see stars dropping from God's sky to cling to his turban so hard that they blended into its ornaments.

I had never in my life seen a souq. The one shop in al-Awafi, and the festival sweet biscuits laid out on wooden planks at the edge of the space where religious ceremonies were always held – that was all I knew. The Ibri souq was simply a corridor of facing shops, or perhaps these were more like warehouses since I couldn't see any merchants inside, waiting for customers. They sat on mats on the ground or on the stone benches outside their shops, with various baskets of different sizes lined up before them, carrying a variety of goods: dried dates, spices, dried lemons, red peppers, barley. Sometimes there would also be a tray or two of dried coconut. I'm certain it was those enormous tin platters of dried coconut that preserved my memory of that day so vividly that I can still see it and smell it even now: the souq exactly as it looked then. Closing my eyes, I can see the tree trunks and the arcing date-palm fronds, creating a vault overhead that knitted the two separate rows of shops into one entity. I can see the iron hooks from which wool carpets were hung, and the baskets, leather pelts, reed mats, and even the dried fish whose sharp odour still comes to me instantly. Boys scampered here and there, most often wearing the leather belts that already awaited the daggers they'd receive in days to come. The merchants exchanged news, stared at people indifferently and waved their canes in the air. What drew my gaze was the red colours of their turbans, the jumble of smells, the heaps of coconut. I liked it all.

Directly on the ground sat the barber, ramrod straight, a turban on his head and a dagger in his belt, sleeves rolled up to show his bare forearms. His customer sat down facing him but leaving enough space that he could bend forward slightly, signalling that he was ready to entrust his head to the broadly grinning barber. Unlike the barber, his customer wasn't sitting on bare ground but on a ragged square of rough canvas onto which his shaven hair would fall. The barber had his tools laid out next to him on an ancient wood chest along with a small bucket of water which he sprinkled on the customer's head. When the customer arose it was invariably with a shaven head since this barber had no experience actually cutting hair. All he could do was shave it to the roots.

I don't know what roused all of those smells in me as Mayya and I stood on the verge watching. A very fine large villa was going up on the plot of land that she had chosen and the municipality had refused to sell to us – the land which was included in the future planning for the governorate's multi-lane highway. Hah! exploded Mayya. So the land was sold after all! What happened to the city planning, to the document signed by the Cabinet? How much will the municipality pay now to change the fast line's route, now that they've given in so very respectfully to the demands of whoever it was who wanted this land for his villa?

I didn't say anything. The smells of the old souq in Ibri filled my lungs.

This headache is affecting my hearing. When I was little, my father's hand on my head could absorb my headache. Laying his hand there, he would repeat the words from the Qur'an: To Him belongs everything that rests quietly, in the night as by day. My head would grow quiet, at rest, and the pain would go away.

But my father's veined hand swelled under the intravenous needles in the Nahda Hospital and could no longer reach for my head, splitting in pain, unable to give way to sleep.

The hand of Bill, the English teacher, was not heavily

veined. It was covered with minute freckles. It was Bill who convinced me I must learn English. We met at a dinner party organised by one of the Muscat merchants. In serviceable Arabic, Bill queried me. You are a businessman and you don't know English? No restaurant in Muscat will serve you if you don't have any language! He was right. And I was tired of the acute embarrassment I felt whenever I tried to reserve a hotel room, or was invited to dinner at a restaurant. In my own country! My Arab country, where restaurants, hospitals and hotels all announced that 'only English is spoken here'.

I started private lessons with Bill. His blue eyes gave nothing away but his smile seemed promising. Before getting to know him I would never have imagined that a person's smile could reveal his intelligence, but Bill's smile gave form to a shrewd mind.

My father did not smile. Or perhaps he did smile, a little, once in a very great while. If his mouth did begin to curve I would feel instant contentment, but the sparky brilliance his eyes gave off awakened only my terror. I would never be that smart, no matter how much I studied or learned. I would always be the gullible little boy, or the deluded lad who would never know how to manage the family business and would never have his papa's brains. That astute gaze, that smile hinting such cleverness – I search in my children's faces, but I never see my father's expressions there. London? Perhaps, if only she hadn't gotten mired in Ahmad's lies.

Whenever I think of that whole affair I feel so angry that I almost can't breathe. When Mayya discovered they were talking, she smashed London's mobile, locked her in her room, and slapped her as she had never slapped anyone before. After, she remained on high alert, ready to detect the slightest vibration in the air. But stubborn London insisted on her love. Why does it still pain me so much? After all, it is over, isn't it? Does it hurt because I gave in to her, allowing the two of them to sign a marriage contract? Or because I didn't support her, didn't stand up for her love, from the very beginning? Or because I scolded her for choosing him, but only after it went bad? Am I hurting because he harmed her? Or is it because Mayya never knew love and so she did not know, when London fell in love, how to deal with her daughter?

Didn't you at least have some notion of what love is, Mayya? Didn't you feel something of what I went through as I paced around your family home like a pilgrim circles the Kaaba, once, twice, seven times?

How could the house ever be spacious enough to hold all of my passion? How did its single balcony bear up under me, as I stood there alone, weighted down by so much love, without collapsing onto the dirt street or fragmenting, to be carried off by the breezes into God's heavens? How did the small room bear the tons of clouds I kept stored away in there, simply so that I could walk across them? How did the walls stay still and unshakeable, never once quaking with the torment of my unbearable joy?

But everything remained in its place even if I had no place. The doors did not fly off their hinges even if my cast down body was riddled with the live bullets of desperate love. The windows did not shatter, though my wings beat hard against the glass, strong enough to soar from the front window to the furthest speck on the horizon. The house was roomy enough to hold me, to contain the scream of desire that echoed inside me.

Then how could it be, Mayya, that your eyes, fixed on your sewing machine, never could see the vast and tortuous expanse of my love, and my imprisoned self?

Asma

Still drowsy, Asma opened her eyes slowly. Seconds later, she remembered that today was her wedding day. She stretched, pressed her hands against her stomach, and smiled at the thought that a few months from now it might well be rounded and full. Getting up, she folded up her bedding, hung it on the peg and hurried to the kitchen. Her father liked to have his coffee as soon as he'd come from dawn prayers.

Asma found her mother sitting on the worn steps leading into the kitchen. Salima's distracted air startled her daughter. She never allowed herself to lose composure, even momentarily; Asma had often wondered how she could do it. Wishing her good morning, her mother's voice came faintly. In the kitchen the coffee was already bubbling on the flame, the cardamom ready next to it.

Something was wrong but Asma couldn't figure out what it was. Her father drank his usual two cups of coffee and glanced at her as he gnawed on the dates that invariably began his day. Asma didn't feel uncomfortable or embarrassed, as perhaps was expected of her on such a day, but she did sense some kind of silent rebuke in his eyes. It set off a vague feeling of remorse, or perhaps of guilt, but again, she couldn't identify what the problem was.

On her mother's orders she shut herself in her room. No one must see the bride before her wedding. Mayya had been in seclusion for an entire week and not a single woman from the neighbourhood had gotten a glimpse of her before the evening of her wedding. Asma breathed out a long sigh. Praise be to God that her mother hadn't insisted on isolating her for a whole week! All Salima had done was to forbid Asma to leave the house, but that was more or less in effect all the time, anyway, so it seemed a bit of a joke as a maternal ruling for the week preceding the wedding. Did she want Asma to know the value of the freedom that marriage would give her? She'd be one of the women now, and finally she would have the right to come and go, to mix freely with the older women and listen to their talk, to attend weddings, all of them, near and far, and funerals too. Now she would be one of the women who sat around their coffee in the late mornings and then again at the end of the day. She would be invited to lunch and dinner, and she would issue her own invitations, since she was no longer merely a girl. Marriage was her identity document, her passport to a world wider than home.

When younger, she had always eagerly welcomed the date harvest as an opportunity to go out and enjoy herself with the other girls. Early in the morning they would walk outside al-Awafi to the farms, moving from one to the next, inspecting the ripening dates as they were separated, cleaned and sorted. The girls could play with the unripe red ones and splash around in the moving water that the canal system sent from one field to the next, according to a fixed water distribution schedule which guaranteed strict fairness. But the greatest fun awaited them at the end of the day, in the open space amidst the farms where the faaghuur was made. She had always found it a captivating sight, Asma remembered: the stream of unripe dates pouring into the enormous cauldrons of boiling water. She and her friends competed to guess which one would be ready first. At that point, the men removed the hot mass with palm-fibre ladles, spreading it out in the sun so that it would dry, whereupon it would be packed and shipped to Muscat where government buyers purchased it for export to India. Asma didn't like its taste, preferring dates that were fresh. People in al-Awafi bit into faaghuur only to test that they'd gotten it right and certainly not for any other reason. Not when they could eat ripe dates. Asma and her friends spent the entire harvest day running around in play, shimmying up the smaller palm trees and swinging from palm-fibre ropes tied between two trunks. They delighted in annoying the women working in the fields, picking through the dates they would carry back at the end of the day in large bundles on their heads, or collecting the rotting dates left behind, filling large sacks that they would drag away to feed to their sheep or to sell to others who owned sheep. Asma could remember how she had ripped a hole in Fattum's sackcloth without Fattum knowing it. As she walked, the rotten dates falling from her sack traced a long line behind her. For days afterward, Asma's friends laughed at the image of it. But Asma had grown up. She no longer went to the harvest games. Now she didn't even go out for the first day of the month of Dhu al-Hijja to sing with her friends.

Muhammad has come down to the wadi
without any water or food
Muhammad has come to paradise now
And the houris' daughters are after him.
My greetings and prayers I've given the Prophet
My greetings and prayers to the Messenger

On this morning it wasn't long before the house was echoing with the voices of the women who had come to carry her trousseau to the groom's home. They filled the pickup that Emigrant Issa had rented from a Bedouin. Asma's two cases and her mandus went in, along with the embroidered pillows and two Persian carpets. The first case carried her new clothes. The second one hardly held anything but the bottle of French perfume, the aloes-wood oil and the varieties of incense her mother had selected. But her mother insisted on the two cases anyway, as a sign to all that her daughter's trousseau was generous and worthy.

Mayya went along with the women to arrange her sister's belongings in her new home, which Asma had not yet seen. The bride remained behind her firmly closed door with Khawla and a neighbour woman who was in charge of the crucial matter of henna. Thoughts of motherhood, her new clothes, the women dancing, and what it would be like to leave her childhood home had all wandered through Asma's mind, but she hadn't given a thought to Khalid, her long-awaited bridegroom. A few weeks before, when her mother had informed her of the engagement, she had considered the matter calmly and given her consent.

When she and her father quoted poetry at each other, each one trying to outdo the other, Asma sometimes repeated lines of love poetry, or if she didn't, her father did. She always read to him in the winter evenings, especially from the collection of poetry by the great word artist al-Mutanabbi. They would smile together at the opening lines of his odes, on the lover's grief at his beloved's absence, and his longing. But she was not as attached to the Arabic tradition of love poetry, with its flights of coy fancy, as her father was. Nor was she particularly drawn to the love scenes in the few novels she had read. A friend of hers found these at a small bookstore in Muscat but when Asma tried to read them she found them too unrealistic and foreign to interest her. The last novel she had read was something called *Secrets of the Palace* which took place in eighteenth-century France. It was all about royal passions – pleasure, betrayal, mirth. Asma didn't find it convincing. She preferred what she considered more realistic books. But the one text she had found truly memorable and compelling was the passage she had memorised without even really understanding what it meant. Something about spirits or souls that were perfectly round once upon a time but had been split apart. For as long as they were separated they would search out their other half until they found it. That is how she imagined love: a meeting of spirit-twins. She certainly never imagined experiencing a love so fierce that her nights would stretch as long as the nights of the lovers in al-Mutanabbi's poems, or nights filled with worries and cares like Imru' l-qays's nights. She wanted to marry someone who stood out from others, a different order of being, but who would also give her a sense of security and ordinariness. She would love him, of course, and she could have the motherhood she wanted so much.

Her heart was vacant enough, so why would it not open up for Khalid? She did confess to herself that she'd noticed Marwan, the cousin of her sister Mayya's husband. She had seen him on a few occasions, and each time, she was taken with the sense of tranquil purity that this figure in white radiated, a silhouette who hardly spoke a word. In fact it was his mysteriousness that ignited her dreams. She was aware that her glimpses of him had been few. Anyway, on the last feast day when he had come to pay his respects to the family, she'd been a bit frightened by the expression in his eyes. She didn't understand her feelings but she knew his gaze scared her. There was something odd beneath the surface of his silence. She stopped thinking about him.

Khalid... Khalid, the horse artist. He was certainly someone out of the ordinary, as she had fancied. His father, Issa, had acquired his nickname of 'Emigrant' by leaving Oman for Egypt in 1959 after the defeat of Imam Ghalib al-Hina'i in the war of the Jabal al-Akhdar. Like nearly two thousand other Omani families who fled, fearing the English and their ruthless manipulations of power, Issa hoisted the burden of his little family onto his shoulders and settled them and himself in Cairo. His sons Khalid and Ali finished their educations there, and his daughter Ghaliya was born there. When Oman's new government offered an amnesty in the 1970s, asking the fugitives to return and share in constructing a new awakening for a united Oman, Issa the Emigrant refused the offer outright, his head high in exile.

But when Ghaliya grew sick, and then when she died, her mother insisted that they must bury her in her ancestral town. Khalid had just graduated from the Fine Arts Academy so he returned with his parents to the place he had left as a boy. Ali stayed in Cairo to finish his degree and to see out some family obligations. Then he too returned to a town he barely remembered from childhood. Now here they were seeking marriages with hometown girls, these sisters, Asma and Khawla.

A long genealogy connected the two families but what mattered were the few holiday encounters. Asma and Khalid had spoken occasionally. Once she even saw his paintings, on the one family visit to their home that her mother allowed her to join. She was astonished to see such an overwhelming number of paintings all on the same theme, all of the same image. Horses.

Ali's paintings were precise and detailed, capturing every nuance of a horse's build. His steeds barely skimmed the ground, as if they were taking off in flight. Studying these horse-forms, Asma was increasingly certain that the paintings contained within them some kind of disquiet. The images made her anxious; she wished these horse-figures were more firmly planted on the ground. No wonder, years later, she felt drawn to paintings of barefoot women with sturdy legs and feet, images that redressed the unease that had collected inside of her as she gazed at the horses – so light, fragile, transitory – in her husband's paintings. Solid chunky bare legs; she found them reassuring.

Issa the Emigrant was straightforward with her father. We want Asma and Khawla for Khalid and Ali. They'll live with us in Muscat. Anyone who has lived for a long period in a city like Cairo can't endure life in a tiny backwater like al-Awafi.

For Asma, moving to Muscat meant she could continue her studies and get a degree. She would enrol in one of the city's secondary schools and maybe after that she could even get admitted to the university that people said was under construction, or one of the colleges that already existed. She could go on learning. She recalled her mother's story about her grandfather Shaykh Masoud, the one with the library. A smart, quick boy with a love of knowledge, he wanted to go to the Saidiyya School in Muscat. But his father decided that life in Muscat posed too much of a danger for a future head of the tribe. So the boy learned what he learned from shaykhs and imams in mosques, moving between the centres of learning that existed then in Nazwa and al-Rustaq, though he never forgot his dream of going to modern schools. Later on, he worked with some others on founding a modern school. They wanted to locate it in an open city on the coast, and they chose Sur. After a flurry of planning they laid the foundations but then orders were issued from on high: they were to do no more. In the 1940s the mere idea of educating Omanis terrified the rulers. Masoud and his friends learned of one senior bureaucrat's reaction, expressed in an exchange with an English confidante, which said it all: Are we going to educate Omanis like you educated the Indians, and so they revolted against you, and soon they'll oust you entirely?

So the school project in Sur came to an early and rapid close. Masoud returned to his books, procured from India, Egypt and the Arab capitals at the eastern end of the Mediterranean. Salima, telling Asma about her grandfather, didn't really know how to explain her father's determination when it came to studies. But Asma thought she knew what he must have felt. She said quietly to her mother: The longing to know things consumes people sometimes. It was a desire that consumed her as it had her grandfather, despite the many years that separated them.

Salima

When the truck took Asma's wedding things away her mother collapsed, alone in the big front room. She felt pangs of hunger, that most familiar of sensations from her childhood, all the time she was growing older, crouched at the foot of the kitchen wall in her uncle's fortress-like compound, denied the bounties of its kitchen. True, she had not spent her childhood stirring big pots or sweeping or carrying water or wood on her head. True, she was not a slave or a servant. But nor had she ever had the satisfaction of a full stomach or the pleasures of wearing pretty clothes or learning embroidery, since Shaykh Said was not her father but only her father's brother. She couldn't leave the confines of the walled compound or play with the girls who lived nearby. She didn't have a part in the shared laughter and play when women and girls were bathing in the falaj, nor in the dancing at weddings like the girls from slave families did. She couldn't be given remnants of old clothes out of which she could make gowns for wooden dolls. But equally, she didn't have gold chains or bracelets to put on, nor could she enjoy the delicacies of the table like the daughters of shaykhs did. She grew up at the foot of the kitchen wall, always hungry, always observing slave women's freedom to live and dance, and mistress women's freedom to command others, adorn themselves as they liked, and make visits to their likes in other well-off families.

She could certainly remember the visits her mother made to her and Muaadh, every one surreptitious, their mama cowed. When Mama came to see them her eyes were always puffy. She held them and mumbled words they couldn't really hear. They knew how she begged Shaykh Said time after time to let them live with her, in her brother's home. But he always said the same thing. He would not abandon his brother's children, allowing them to be raised by virtual strangers, outsiders to their father's big and important family.

Salima particularly remembered a visit when she had just turned ten years old. Instead of sitting with her in the courtyard, half-hidden under the kitchen wall, her mother led her to a room inside her uncle's forbidding home. She unrolled her head wrap which had been knotted into a bundle. Undoing the knot she took out several pairs of silver earrings and a needle. She smiled at her daughter, telling her that after a lot of difficulty and toil she'd come up with the money to buy these earrings, just for her. From this day on, declared her mother, Salima would be every bit as grand as her uncle's daughters. Pulling Salima onto her lap, she poked the needle into a pounded clove of garlic to purify it and then plunged it repeatedly into Salima's ear, making at least ten holes from the top of her ear lobe all the way down. The little girl's tears soaked her mother's lap as she submitted herself to the pain. Her mother strung black threads through every hole. Two days later, after the swelling had gone down, her mother came back. She took out the threads and put in the silver earrings, a set of graduated rings, increasing in size and heaviness the lower they were on her ear. Her mother was very proud, and Salima could see that. She endured the terrible pains that wearing these heavy earrings caused. Her ears swelled and festered to the point that she couldn't sleep on her side, not on either side. She spent countless nights awake, trying to fall asleep on her stomach with her chin against the hard floor. By the time she felt better, some weeks later, and got used to the heaviness of the silver earrings, she'd come to hate any sort of jewellery, indeed any and all of the ways women prettied themselves up.

Abdallah

Zarifa squats on the ground and her enormous breasts spill onto her lap as her plump fingers, heavy with silver rings, undo the taping around the little cartons of finest-quality Omani jelly-sweet. She taps the almond garnish and dark brown surface lightly, and it quivers. Just have a look at that sweet sight! All this goodness, then they say to me, Don't eat it, remember your diabetes, it's all sugar, leave it. Well, sugar or no sugar, sorry, Zarruuf doesn't leave sweets alone. All sugar, they'll grumble, well, hah! Zarifa picks up a large chunk and crams it into her mouth with all her fingers, and makes a point of licking them, as if now, at this moment, she's getting her sweet revenge for those many years of hunger she knew in the household of Shaykh Said, before my father bought her.

Hide me away in your soft warm chest, Zarifa – I am frightened. Hold my head, rest it somewhere between your lap and your breasts. Let me breathe in your sweat and the smell of broth you always carry, and then, let me sleep. I am afraid, Zarifa. My father won't forgive me for your death. My father will never relent, and I am afraid of what he will do. He's come out of his grave, again and again, to question me about you. He tied me up with that palm-fibre rope, do you remember, and he threw me upside down into the well.

From the bottom of the well, I shouted. She died a peaceful death, the Lord took her away, long after your time. You'd already been dead for years.

But he did not raise me out of the well.

He left me there, head down in the pitch-black well shaft.

As God is great, Father, I did not even know! I'd moved to Muscat by then and the business consumed every moment. I only went back to al-Awafi for feast days. I heard she'd come back from Kuwait. They said she couldn't stand living with Shanna. Somebody said Shanna threw her out of the house, and somebody else claimed she tried to get Zarifa locked up as a madwoman, so Zarifa fled. Still others said that Zarifa just missed al-Awafi too much and couldn't endure being away. That she saw her mother Ankabuta in a dream, calling her, so she came back. She moved in with relatives.

Father, I was so busy. It was just after the stock market collapsed, and Abu Salih and I were trying desperately to build up our business. Father, I was so busy, all of the time. I was in Muscat, and I was in al-Khuwayr, al-Ghubra, I was in al-Hayl, Sib, I was in every single town and area anywhere near Muscat, I was searching for a bit of land, a house, a villa, contractors, a clinic that could help us with Muhammad's autism, English-language institutes, accounting classes, a car bigger than your old white Mercedes, any good deals, a decent travel agent, reliable domestic servants – Philippinas, Indonesians – schools for the children, tutors, a driver, places to spend the evening, friends . . .

My father did not lift me out of the well.

Pull, Father! Haul up the rope. Tug hard on the end you are holding until the other end tightens around my waist enough that I come up. The well is dark, Father, and snakes live in here. Lift me out, I won't steal your rifle, I won't go off with Marhun and Sanjar, anyway, Sanjar is working as a porter in the souk now, Father, and Shanna works as a school janitor. Zarifa is the one who left, she left them, she couldn't stand life in Kuwait.

Get me out of this well, Father. I won't be longing for those magpies and I won't play ball with the boys. I won't stay up late listening to the bewitching melodies of Suwayd's oud, I won't scream into your face, and you in a coma, that Sanjar ran away just like his father, Habib, and that I'm the only one who didn't run away. Raise me out of here, I won't leave Zarifa, your beloved, your mother, your daughter, your slave, your lady. I won't leave her to die alone in some forgotten hospital.

The diabetes got worse, Father, it was terrible. Do you know what it means, the sukkari? It went through her whole body, it was horrible, and they amputated her leg. Her relatives said, We aren't going to keep supporting a crippled woman. Then they cut off her other leg and the neighbours said, Who is going to take her to the bathhouse? Who is going to drag this enormous body with no legs over there? The hospital director was kind. He let her stay in there for good, and the nurses took care of her.

Hoist me up, Father.

Zarifa, bring me up from this well.

I'm afraid.

I am so, so afraid.

Azzan and Qamar

Azzan brought her close. Najiya! My Fullest Moon, I want you, mine.

I am yours, Najiya whispered. Already.

He moaned. No, not completely. Others are always other.

She slipped out of his grip. What do you mean?

I mean, people are always apart, Najiya, they're separate in the end, even when they think they're one. It's the harshest kind of aloneness there is.

She gave him a disapproving look and at that, he grinned. Do you remember Ibn al-Rumi?

Now Najiya smiled. The pessimist? Yes, of course.

He hugged her close again. Do you know what he says?

Though I hold her close, my soul still yearns
yet how can I be closer than in her embrace?
I kiss her mouth to chase my fever away
but my mad cast-off love-thirst burns ever more
The reach of my passion! May that craving be cured
by the sweetness of that which my lips do absorb
My exposed weathered heart will never heal itself
until these two selves are seen as one mingled

At the same instant the two of them sighed.

Those poets who sang about the pleasure of possession weren't lovers, he said flatly. They were hunters.

Najiya's smile turned lightly sarcastic. Hunters?

Yes, that's right, Azzan said firmly. A lover, Najiya, doesn't possess the beloved, however much pleasure the lover feels, and however close to the beloved. A true beloved is like you – someone who can't be owned.

Najiya looked uneasy. She'd never known how to hide her feelings, and it made her especially uncomfortable that Azzan was spoiling their togetherness with words like these. Why did he have to start talking about ownership? He was the one who had a family, children – and she wasn't demanding anything of him. She was perfectly happy like this. It didn't occur to her to think about things like 'possession' and 'hunting'. Her desire was to be his lover and she was, and she didn't want anything else. Why did he always appear so tortured by cryptic feelings that she couldn't grasp?

The Bridal Procession

Asma planted herself in front of the mirror, imitating Khawla. The figure she stared at was a young woman of middling height, barely twenty years old, with wide brown eyes and a short nose. Her eyelashes felt heavy – all those layers of mascara – and the red lipstick she thought made her face look like a clown's. She glanced quickly over her body, squeezed into the wedding gown picked out by the two mothers together, its glossy, glittery, form-fitting dishdasha with its generous embroidery at the throat and down the long sleeves, as well as the length of the train. Traces of the indeterminate anxiety she'd felt earlier returned. She tried to distract herself by studying the elaborate henna designs that scrolled along the back of her hands and around onto the palms. She glanced into the mirror again and smiled nervously at the sight of her bosom, so high and prominent under the close-fitting gown. She remembered how frightened she had been, a few years ago, when the first visible traces of femininity had taken her by surprise. She had loathed seeing the derisory swelling on her chest and every evening she prayed that by morning it would be gone. Then, and for the next few months, she submitted to her sister Mayya's advice on how to hide this new protuberance. On that evening as she listened to Asma crying at the falaj where they were washing clothes as it grew dark, Mayya said, Don't be so scared, Asma. It's just a new fatty bulge. If you give it a good rub with some salt dissolved in warm water it will melt away. If it's really stubborn like mine was, I'll take in all your undershirts, they'll push it all back and no one will see any of it. But, wearing her altered undershirts, sometimes Asma couldn't breathe because they were so tight. And all the salt did was to make her small chest peel, and it kept on growing anyway, until her mother ordered her to start wearing a head wrap. She taught Asma how to wrap it around her head and neck leaving some fabric so that it would cover her chest too. Once again she could breathe freely, and she stopped saying those special, pleading nightly prayers.

Now, Asma lowered her eyes to stare at her stomach, flat and taut in the mirror. She couldn't keep back a grin as she imagined it rounding out. And then, as soon as it was vacated, she hoped, it would grow big and round again. She didn't have a specific number of children in mind – it was hard to imagine any of this, really – but she could see herself vaguely as an old woman standing beside an aged Khalid as dozens of sons and daughters and grandchildren gathered around them.

She looked the mirror-figure in the eye, and both of them shivered. It was the thought that she was about to join the other half of her, the self which had been separated from her self ever since earliest creation. In her mind she recited that favourite passage of hers, describing how humans were only halves of a whole, long ago detached one from the other, and no half could be truly complete or at peace until it was united with its missing part. What was Khalid feeling right now? Was he as anxious as she was? Was he feeling happy? Oh! Despite all of these worried thoughts she could not wait for them to be together.

At sunset, women began to descend in groups on Salima's house. They crowded around the huge platters of rice and meat, and the trays of fruit, that sat on cloths stretched across the courtyard. Singing and the sound of drums rose, and the circles of dancers expanded. Zarifa joined the group dancing the hambura. The bridegroom's mother arrived with a group of kinswomen in tow, their gleeful shouts adding to the mayhem. We want our bride! Give us our bride! They didn't tarry, turning immediately toward Asma, a seated silhouette draped in a green silk shawl. Salima helped her to her feet and hugged her before manoeuvering her arm into the grasp of the groom's mother, who marched her proudly to the decked-out bright red Mercedes that was waiting at the door, Emigrant Issa himself at the wheel. All the women followed the procession out, climbing into the buses ordered specially for the wedding. They would follow the bridal car all the way to Muscat and the flat Khalid had rented as a bridal retreat, and their new home.

With the bridal procession's departure a sudden stillness fell over the house, sending fear into Salima's heart. She collapsed on the reception-room steps. Here was the second of her girls leaving the house, and this was the daughter who tried her tenderness the most. We raise them so that strangers can take them away, she whimpered. She left everything just as it was; in the morning, there would be people here to help her clean and put everything right. Now, though, everyone was caught up in the ongoing singing and dancing, first in the buses and then at the groom's home. She wished she could be there when Khalid lifted the silk shawl from Asma's face, but she respected the tradition that the mother of the bride does not go to the groom's home on her daughter's wedding day. In the middle room, where she had slept ever since Azzan abandoned her bed, she rolled out her bedding and lay down, still thinking about Asma, and suddenly overwhelmed, too, by memories of her own wedding and the day she was taken to Azzan's home.

She was thirteen when her uncle Shaykh Said's wife urged him in no uncertain terms to send her to her mother now. But only after his brother's widow begged him one final time did Shaykh Said agree that Salima could live with her, on condition that Muaadh remained in his house. So Salima moved to her maternal uncle's home, where she spent the loveliest years of her life, enjoying her mother's warmth and her maternal uncle's affection. Her mother's brother had not been blessed with children and he welcomed her with open arms. His home was nicknamed Orchard House because it was a tangle of fruit trees and bushes – mango, lemon, orange, quince, jasmine, roses. The rooms had been built in a crescent shape to accommodate the trees. This small orchard was the centre of the house, its pivot onto which every room opened. The fresh, moist breezes that this unique building let in soon filled Salima's spirit. She especially loved sinking her feet into the series of small canal-streams that kept the orchard watered, flowing into a larger underground channel that went on for several metres before pouring into al-Awafi's main canal.

Salima's rapture didn't last long. Very soon her paternal uncle informed her mother that he was going to marry Salima to his kinsman Azzan, a green and heedless boy a few years her senior. Her mother was not keen on this marriage and her own brother took her side. They opposed this match strenuously and persistently, objecting on the grounds that Azzan was still a tender youth, and still a young apprentice-follower of Judge Yusuf's. Moreover, they insisted, it was very possible that he would decide to follow the family members who had emigrated to Zanzibar, leaving his wife behind. But Shaykh Said put his foot down and warned Salima's maternal uncle that if he didn't open the gate to Orchard House to allow her to leave, he would get her out in his own way. Her mother's brother felt his honour humiliated by this threat. He bolted the front gate.

On the day that Shaykh Said had set for the wedding Salima was eating the midday meal with her mother and uncle when, from the big canal in their orchard, swarmed a cluster of slaves, men and women, who belonged to Shaykh Said. Water dripping from their bodies, they formed a tight circle around the startled, and then terror-stricken, family. Salima had to go with them right now, they said. Otherwise they would have to take her by force, making her swim through the orchard canal to the main falaj outside. At that, her uncle opened the gate. The men and women who had invaded his home took Salima away, and a few hours later she became Azzan's bride. People would go on calling her the Bride of the Falaj for years afterward. Many, very long, years afterward.

Abdallah

Why do people say my grandmother died bewitched? asked London.

Because that's how they explained any death that happened suddenly and any illness they couldn't explain, I responded.

Do you know what she was ill with, Papa? London asked intently.

I don't know, I mumbled.

But I'm a doctor. So maybe I could figure it out. Did anyone tell you what her symptoms were, and how long she was sick?

Yes. People say she got sick very suddenly, two weeks after I was born. Her skin turned blue and her pupils contracted. She started sweating very heavily and she couldn't stop shivering. People said the spirits were fighting it out with each other on her body and that's why she was shaking so hard and giving off so much sweat. Then, they said, the strongest spirit won her from the others, and so she quieted down and got very cold. People assumed she had died so they buried her.

London's face looked very pale. What's wrong? I asked.

These symptoms are common to a number of illnesses but most likely they indicate poisoning, London said, her voice edgy. I remember what Gramma Salima told me, she said a lot of poisonous herbs, like habb al-muluk, and red and yellow dafla, grow in the desert around al-Awafi. She told me that sometimes women slipped traces of these into their co-wives' food to make them ill. Then they'd have the husband to themselves.

I put my arm firmly around her shoulder. London! My mother didn't have any co-wives.

She nodded her head. Yes, that's true. Where was my grandfather at the time?

On a trip to Salalah for his trade. That's why no one took her to Thomas, the American missionary who was famous because he treated people's illnesses without taking any money. People lined up from dawn until late at night to see him.

It's very odd, muttered London. They could be symptoms of another illness ... maybe ... who knows?

I couldn't sleep that night. Everyone had similar things to say about witchery and the jinn. Only Zarifa never joined in when people talked about my mother's illness. But Zarifa was dead now. Did questions like these have anything to do with her insistence on tasting every dish before I ate from it, all through my childhood? I don't know ... I don't know ... How would I know, anyway?

Azzan and Qamar

As the last drumbeats sounded at Asma's wedding Azzan was rolling about on the cool sand with Najiya. He stared into her face – the most beautiful sight he had seen in his life – and recited some lines by al-Mutanabbi that had come to him just then.

I stake my word on the desert gazelle and what she's free of –
no slur in her speech nor pencilled-on eyebrows
The faces of city girls seen as pretty are nothing
to the faces of the Bedouin, those ra'aabib
What passes for handsome in the eyes of settled folk
happens with perfumes and padding but nomad
girls need none.

Najiya's deep laughter rocketed through the desert silence. That's your friend, the one called al-Mutanabbi, the one you told me about?

Yes, he's the one, Najiya, Azzan replied with a sigh.

She started laughing again. So, what are these ra'aabib he talks about?

Azzan sat up and brushed the sand off. A ra'buba, Najiya,

is a woman with a gorgeously full body. And the gazelle of the desert – that's you.

Oh, really. She sounded annoyed. Do I chew my words, then, like a gazelle chews her cud?

You chew my heart, Najiya. Aah, Najiya, Judge Yusuf – may God's mercy surround him – used to talk to me about hearts. On and on he would go, and I didn't understand any of what he was saying. Now I think I do understand it all.

All?

Azzan, my boy! Judge Yusuf would say. Your name is a word that holds secrets – it is a secret in itself. Listen – the first letter in your name, ayn, is a cold letter in the fourth degree, and it holds two levels of cold moisture, which is the first of the secrets of the throne, the ‘arsh, which also begins with the letter ayn, just like your name. Ayn is the first of its letters and the first of the worlds it invented – and worlds, awalim, starts with ayn too. Your name holds the cosmos, Azzan.

Najiya didn't understand any of this. Hearing Judge Yusuf's name didn't bring her any comfort, either. But Azzan went on.

When he married Maryam, he told me, his heart was no longer just a mirror in which the beauty of the universe shone, like it was before. Now his heart was completely taken up by Maryam and the children. One time he mentioned to me that he regretted having ignored the advice of the great master al-Ghazali, who told *his* disciple to keep well away from marriage. To refuse it when his family insisted, to turn it down in the time of its asking, when his family presented it as his work in the world.

Is this Ghazali the fellow who wrote the book that turns readers insane? Najiya grumbled. Who is this disciple, and what does that mean, in the time of its asking?

God show you his mercy, Judge Yusuf! When that man

died not even a single hair on his head had gone white. Al-Ghazali – Najiya, he wrote a lot of books, and they don't make people go insane. But most people don't understand them. They want to be kept happy, to stay comfortable, so they don't usually try to meet all the conditions that someone like al-Ghazali sets for them.

Are you happy and comfortable, Azzan?

He smiled and closed his eyes. How could I be, when my heart is chewed up in your beautiful mouth? How will my heart become a pure mirror, Moon of mine?

I am your mirror.

They fell into silence.

The hills around them were silent. In Azzan's ears echoed remnants of sounds: the drums at his daughter's wedding, Qamar's silver anklets, her laughing that seemed itself a stream of blessed musk, and her stories about the hand-worked fabrics that merchants bought from her to sell to tourists in Matrah. The voices and sounds faded, even al-Mutanabbi's voice, declaring himself to all in a famous line as the voice known to steeds and the night, to the desert and the sword and the spear, to ink and the pen. All the voices, all the sounds became fading circles spinning in his head before they quieted, making room for a single deep voice. Judge Yusuf's voice.

He who faithfully strives to understand and do what is best; who frees himself from excessive appetites and anger and other blameworthy acts and ugly deeds; who sits in a place empty of others and closes the eye of his senses to open the eye of the hidden and to listen; who keeps his heart in the world of God's kingdom, uttering the name of the Almighty, preserving this name in his heart always, and of course on his tongue, until he is no longer a separate being, a person in the world; until he sees naught but God, praise be to His Exaltedness. To this striving person will be opened a window. When he looks through it, a person who is able will perceive more than ordinary folk will. Though he be awake, this discerning person will perceive the stuff of dreams. The spirits of the angels and prophets will come to him, and so will other beautiful and mighty images, the kingdom of heaven and the kingdom of earth. He will have visions that he cannot explain or describe. As our Prophet, peace and blessings be upon him, said: The earth was concealed to me yet I saw its east and its west both. Azzan, if you would be this person, for seven days commit yourself to repeating only the name of God. Fast in the daytime and remain awake for as much of the night as you can. Detach yourself from others; do not speak to a soul, and the wonders of creation will be revealed to you. Do this for a further seven days and you will receive the grace of seeing the wonders of the heavens. Another seven, you will visit the wonders of the highest kingdom. Should you reach forty days God will show you His miracles and impart His hidden knowledge.

Azzan felt a shudder run through his body and sweat covered him. Najiya leaned toward him. What's the matter?

He gave her a look of terror. I must go.

He snatched up his slippers and was gone.

Judge Yusuf, I am afraid. Afraid! My heart's been snatched away and it sits high in the eagles' nest. The black expanses that shadow my heart crowd all of the other images out, I cannot see them in its mirror. I cannot see, Judge Yusuf. I cannot see anything.

Abdallah

Zarifa told me that as a tiny baby I cried endlessly. After her husband made up with her and she went back to him, my aunt wanted to take me with her but my father turned her down flat. He assigned Zarifa to raise me. He bought several milking ewes but their milk wasn't enough to quiet me. So sometimes Zarifa packed my nose with snuff to make me go to sleep. Whenever she sensed me crying because my ears hurt, she poured a few drops of coffee into my ear canals. Or she took me to nursing women, asking them to squeeze drops of their milk into my eyes, since she thought I might be crying because my eyes hurt. When I was a little bigger she strung amulets around my neck to protect me from envy and convinced my father to pierce my ears so she could hang silver earrings there. What she called the night-folk might not recognise that I was a boy and snatch me away just as they had kidnapped my mother. She embroidered the caps I wore with her own hands. It certainly didn't diminish her pride that on feast days I was the only child in al-Awafi who wore slippers and a jubba decorated with tiny mirror-sequins procured from India.

Zarifa would recount all of this, chuckling. She raised me until the coming of The Great Anger as she called it, the massive argument between her and my father; I never learned the causes of it. He punished her by abandoning her and then marrying her off to the most eccentric and aggressive slave he had, Habib, who was at least ten years her junior.

London

The buses coming from Asma and Khalid's wedding were back in al-Awafi just before dawn. The women's passion for song and dance had given way to exhaustion, and some of them had fallen asleep. Mayya, though, sat wide awake next to the window. Everything, all of it, had seemed like a dream sequence. Without any warning, she had been married to the son of Merchant Sulayman. Next, her sister was married to the son of Issa the Emigrant. Her youngest sister Khawla was still waiting – waiting for her cousin Nasir.

During Asma's wedding festivities, she had whispered, over and over: Lord, bring Nasir back to me. Everyone knew that Nasir wasn't coming back. But stubborn Khawla would not listen to anyone.

Mayya stared out the window at the hills still half-submerged in darkness, and tightened her arms around her baby daughter, only a few months old. If that was it, simply, if life was a dream, when would anyone wake up? She stroked her little one and whispered her name almost silently. London … London. Will you be happy, my baby darling?

Barely twenty years later London would be a new divorcee, extracting herself from a marriage contract though not yet in her marital home. With the divorce finalised she began struggling with all of the difficult-to-untangle emotions that bruised her sense of self-respect – an incalculable blend of longing, fury, antagonism and regret. She was certain she would never again be that person she had been before. What people called 'an experience' was in reality a chronic disease, surely – not one you can die from, but not one that is ever cured. Not one you ever really manage; you're never free of it, either. Wherever you go it comes along with you, and it's liable to erupt at any moment, reminding you of consequences it carries that you were either unaware of or were diligently ignoring. And the advice people give us to 'turn the page' is nothing more than a sick joke. London had tried to turn the page on Ahmad. To close that page and open a new one. How many people were doing the same thing, day in and day out?

London, come on! Hanan said to her. Life goes on. Where Ahmad's concerned, just hit Delete, okay? *Let it go*, she said, in English to underline her point. But this page was a heavy one indeed, and trying to turn it, she couldn't keep her hand steady. My God, people are so different. How do other people turn the page? She tried to turn to a new page but she already knew there were no blank pages in life. She'd felt this scar deepening into a wound, her dignity festered and she saw humiliation stamped in the very spot where desire still burned. She arranged her stuffed teddy bears against the pillows, sprayed her expensive Gucci perfume around the room, lowered the curtains on Muscat's night-time and tried to sleep but could not.

Her hard gaze turned inward and ripped open her heart. In her mind's eye, her heart was a triangle. When memories began to rise from the base of the triangle, they were so powerful and so disturbing that they shook all three sides of the triangle hard. The words pelted down, all of the words he'd said to her since the very first time she'd encountered him in the lecture hall, and the long telephone conversations too. The sides of the triangle collapsed, pulverised by all the words, and leaving only tiny word-shards in its place. She turned her eyes away but then she couldn't see anything.

Hanan's words echoed, over and over: *Let it go!* As if this were a rewind of some foreign film: he was a treacherous lover and so the heroine left him. When a friend said to her, *Oh dear . . . my dear, let it go!* the heroine forgot him immediately. Bygones were bygones, the heroine turned the page. End of film. So why did London's hand remain frozen in place, letting itself be crushed under the weight of the page, until she could no longer turn it? Why did this pain, obscure but ruthless, squeeze her so hard? Why couldn't she shake this humiliating sensation, desire and failure in equal measure? London thrashed about in the darkness. She couldn't sleep. Or turn the page.

Zarifa

Zarifa returned from Asma's wedding in a state of collapse prompted by all of the dancing, singing and constantly serving guests. But Merchant Sulayman was wide awake and waiting for her. He particularly liked taking her when she had just come back from a wedding, both because she was still in her outside finery and because she carried with her the allure of the new marriage, which excited him. Zarifa wanted badly to get some rest but she gave him what he wanted as quickly as she could and then he did fall asleep.

She thought she would drop off immediately too, but a sense of unease was edging its way into her though she couldn't pin down the source of it. Weddings didn't bring her the pleasure they once had. And, as proud as she could be of how true her dance steps still were, she really had gotten too heavy for such things. Anyway, what more did a wedding really hold for her than the endless service she had to give to the women who were there as guests? Constantly supplying them with food and drink, and on top of that, the dancing and singing, and all the gossip as well. There was no real pleasure to be had in weddings any more. Only in zar exorcisms.

Those endless ceremonies intoxicated her, everything from

the grilled meat and the drinking to the heavy and incessant pounding of the drums, until the ecstasy of it all lifted her outside of herself, beyond consciousness and into one sort of trance or another. In such a state she might walk across live coals or lie beneath horses' hooves or roll in the dirt under the careening circles of dancing bodies. Her mother – God be merciful to her mother – had been the zar's Big Mama, the one who decided on when to hold one of these events in the first place, and then who presided over them. She was the medium, after all, the woman in direct contact with the jinn who had attached themselves ruthlessly to the human beings writhing on the hot coals. So let Merchant Sulayman whip her for an absence of two or three days while she was immersed in the zar. Let him accuse her of playing around with one of his slaves, let him curse her mother as the child of generations of runaway slaves! Let him do whatever he might, but she simply couldn't put an end to these raging blistering ecstasies.

Even Habib couldn't keep her from going. She'd leave newborn Sanjar there next to him and slip out silently during the night to join her mother. Habib never did anything to bring himself any pleasure, she told herself, and so he didn't want anyone else to get any joy out of anything. If it weren't for this unmanageable son of his she would have forgotten him completely. He was a lot younger than she was. From his mother he inherited his pale skin and short stature. When he clutched her she felt like she was being held by one of the teenaged sons of Shaykh Said who used to put their hands on her when she was barely a teenager, before Merchant Sulayman bought her. She made her aversion clear in every possible way until Habib left her, before she could cause a total scandal, acting as her mother had done with her own husband, Nasib.

Before long, Habib was gone. She thought she was well rid of him, no longer forced to put up with the way he screamed, from the depths of his sleep, We are free people, free! No longer forced to listen to his ravings about the corpses that were thrown into the sea, the pirates, the eye disease. But here was his son turning out exactly like him. Sanjar, too, would run away before long and her heart would burn with grief. If only she had never had him. It still made her groan to remember the long hours of labour and Sanjar's difficult birth. Her mother tried everything to ease the way. She made Zarifa drink a rotten-smelling viscous oil, followed by water into which was mixed soil from a grave, and then more water, this time collected from the dirt floor of an abandoned and collapsed mosque. She made her drink the dissolved leaves of a lotus tree, and honey over which Judge Yusuf had recited verses from the Qur'an. She even turned Zarifa upside down, so frantic was she by this point. When she despaired completely she said to her daughter, Your grandmother died giving birth. Death is fate. But Zarifa did not die, nor did the baby. Ankabuta stuck her hand up the birth passage, tugged until the bluish flesh appeared, and slapped the shapeless thing several times until life surged into it. She performed the date-in-the-mouth ritual, tossed the baby into Habib's hands, and buried the afterbirth under the threshold after smearing it with ashes and salt. She sprinkled the soft sand around exhausted Zarifa with water, gave her fenugreek and clarified butter to drink, placed a knife at her head to ward off any evil magic that might be making its way to her or the baby, and went home to sleep after a vigil that had gone on for several nights.

Still awake at dawn, she asked herself who she had been, the grandmother who died giving birth? Zarifa knew almost nothing about the generations before her. She'd heard it said that her father's mother had run away. That was all she knew. Questions about them had never particularly plagued her in the past and they didn't much occupy her now, though now and then she did think she could see the little African village in which her great-grandfather had spent his nights in peace before it was written that he and his offspring after him would be thrown into entirely different lives?

As Senghor was being born in a small Kenyan village, the Sayyid, Said bin Sultan, was signing a second pact with Britain to ban the slave trade. In the 1885 accords, Sayyid Said had already agreed to put an end to the commerce in slaves that moved between his African and Asian dominions. He had consented to allowing British naval ships to stop and search Omani vessels, even in Omani territorial waters, and throughout the Arabian Gulf and the Indian Ocean. They were to seize and sequester any vessels violating the accords. But Senghor wasn't even quite twenty when he was gone after by pirates from other, more powerful villages. Under cover of darkness they slipped into the dense forests around the village and set up their traps. When Senghor went out at dawn to gather some firewood he fell into a trap and it snapped shut, caging him in. They seized him immediately and took him back to their village along with the other captives, their harvest for the day.

The new slaves were assembled at Kalwa and loaded onto a ship headed for Zanzibar. It was a three-day trip but there was nothing to eat or drink. By the time they arrived at a clandestine collection point on the shore near the harbour, sixty slaves had died, their bodies pitched overboard. The waiting merchants – some were Arabs, some Africans – had paid the head tax, two dollars apiece. The ship emptied its cargo of slaves onto the shore to await the native Sur boats that would sail from the port of Zanzibar. As they waited the merchants seized their opportunity to strike bargains with certain English plantation owners, who returned to their farms with their own bounty: more than one hundred slaves.

A few days later the Sur boat left port, the captain having

sold its cargo of dried fish. Evading the British naval ships, at the secret coastal collection point it took on board the remaining human cargo, those still alive who had not been bought by the Englishmen, Senghor among them. He began to suffer from hallucinations. The ship captain kept a heap of French flags in his cabin; he had acquired from the French authorities in Aden. He had them raised high above deck as a ploy to avoid inspection from any British ships he might encounter unexpectedly in the sea lanes. And so the boat arrived safely at Sur harbour at the end of August, carried by the seasonal gusts of wind coming from the southeast. Senghor had recovered from his hallucinatory spells and the seasickness by then, and had begun to learn Arabic.

The merchants in Sur got to work dividing up the slaves, their argumentative bargaining lasting through the night. Having once again taken full advantage of the clash of interests between Britain and France, the boat captain hid his flags away carefully in his cabin and went home happy. The next morning when the merchants had come to an agreement, the slaves were transported in groups to shacks of two or three floors. With some others Senghor went up to the higher rooms. The windows were merely long slits but they allowed air in from all directions. Though the ground floor was meant for storage, some of the more troublesome slaves were deposited there.

At night the heat was still unbearable. The slaves were permitted onto the roof to sleep in the open air. Even with the breeze off the sea the air was stifling. Senghor tried to counter it by pouring water repeatedly over his body. His eyes were red but he did not cry. He no longer thought about the past, or the future. All he wanted was to sleep on firm ground.

A few days later Senghor was placed with a small group who were sent to the east coast where farm workers were needed. He didn't stay long, for he was sold to a shaykh in al-Awafi. There, Senghor worked in the house and on the farm too. He married one of the shaykh's slave women. When he died at forty of tuberculosis he had had two daughters who died of it too, and a son who married and had sons and a daughter before joining up with a gang of highwaymen and disappearing. His daughter Ankabuta grew up, after her brothers had all been sold away, as an orphan in the home of Shaykh Said. He had just inherited his shaykhly position from his father, although he had barely reached the sixteenth year of what would be a very long life.

Asma and Khalid

When his bride Asma recited the words she'd memorised as a child, about restless souls in search of their departed halves, Khalid had simply remarked, You found that in an old Arabic book? *The Dove's Necklace*, likely.

The Dove's Necklace? Asma repeated. Who wrote a book with such a lovely title?

He gave her a rather lofty smile. An Andalusian legal scholar named Ibn Hazm. I think this is from that book.

Asma leaned towards him eagerly. But do you think it's true, Khalid? That people's souls really were united when the world began, and then were split in half?

He laughed. Asma, it's only an ancient legend. That people were all the same, all one sex, male and female both, all children of the moon. Every being had four hands, four feet and two heads, that's what they said. And then, the gods were afraid that creatures with all of this would be too strong, so they split them in two. Only the belly button remained as a reminder of that original wholeness. People became either one sex or the other. Each half has to search for its other half.

She whispered, Am I your other half, the half that was split off?

He hugged her tightly. The half I have finally found.

He had told her how, just seeing her once, he had fallen in love with her. It wasn't very long, though, before Asma began to realise that people are not simply unmade halves who find their other halves and miraculously become whole. Neither bodies nor spirits are empty globes split down the middle; no pair exists whose souls adhere perfectly like the two identical halves of a perfectly round sphere. Even more disturbing, she began to realise that there was no way she could be Khalid's other half, once upon a time sundered but which (he assured her) he had now found.

This was because Khalid, on his own, took on the likeness of a celestial sphere complete unto itself, orbiting only along its already defined path. Khalid knew exactly what he wanted and now he was getting everything he needed: a fond family, his diploma, and his art which – he made clear to Asma – was at once his inner world and his public work. What had attracted him to Asma – as she gazed wide-eyed at his canvases – was that she fit his needs perfectly. He had already decided on marriage to a woman who would somehow stand out from all the others, with some quality of note. He chose accordingly, looking for a woman who would fall instantly into the orbit he had marked out, who would always be there but would also always stay just outside, yet without wanting to create her own celestial sphere, her own orbit. So he encouraged Asma to continue her education, though at night school because the law now prohibited married women from attending the regular government day schools. He urged her to go on developing her sincere love of reading and when she achieved distinction in her teacher's certificate he encouraged her to get a job. After all, her mature skills and accomplishments would advance his social status, not to mention that they confirmed his confidence in the choices he himself had made. She was a wife one could be proud of, and his acquisition of her put the final touch on his social acceptability. Yes, he had done it: a respectably able wife, circling within his gravitational pull, quietly, invisibly, inside its orbital path, never straying beyond.

It didn't take long for Asma to discover all of this. Nevertheless, she absorbed it calmly and methodically, her feelings already composing an attitude of sceptical affection. Her sentiments were balanced and steady, completely unlike his. At first he was very conscious and careful to adhere to the orbit he had traced out, and he was always checking to be certain that Asma was right there, orbiting in his wake, and watchful above all that she never veered off course. In his own fashion, he did fall in love with her.

As the days passed, his incandescent feelings did not dim, either. He held her high in the firmament. She was a rare wonder, a radiant and translucent butterfly who reflected the light his love generated. She was the flash of perfection that confirmed his sharp sense of the world. But Asma was no butterfly. She wasn't one to dive into the glare only to find herself scorched. She had only to calculate a prudent distance. She had already learned that there were times when the fire would go cold and Khalid would slip away, crawling or perhaps running to his warren, drawing that circle around himself and seemingly forgetting Asma entirely. He might stay inside that impervious little circle of his for days, weeks, sometime months. Then suddenly he would once again become Asma's passionate lover, so much so that his passion tormented her, pulling her inside a hellish paradise, a hard-to-sustain world of absolute pleasures. How ecstatically she blossomed in the early days of his love, astonished that in a matter of days she lived what she had not lived in her whole lifetime before. She loved him with a startling, inexplicable thirst and a craving to feel everything.

Unlike her husband, though, she was not a creature of

impulse. She was not in any hurry to embrace all the joys of love in one gulp of intoxicating ether. As he was growing quiet, her love was pushing its roots deep into the earth, ready to grow, one shoot upon another. At first when he went into his shell Asma was bewildered and upset almost to the point of giving in to her despair. But as time passed and she accumulated experience along with wisdom and social sense, she learned how to accommodate to the situation. She did love him, too – this sceptical, careful, slightly distant love. But she began taking precautions. She formed her own celestial orbit. In the end, and with a great deal of patience, self-examination, and occasional sacrifice, they learned to create enough space that each could orbit freely. When they collided, and if they fused, Asma and Khaled knew it was only a temporary disruption, and that each path would return to its own course.

With the years, children, an accumulation of friends, and her books, Asma made her peace with Khalid's art and self-absorption. She left it alone, the circle he drew round himself, remaining inside contented with nothing more than the wood that would soon receive his paint. She learned patience with his horses: their hard eyes, thin bodies, straining muscles. She could deal with the invariable shades of brown, black and white. She made her peace with it, all of it. In return, the artist had to reconcile himself with the fact that she was her own constellation, independent and whole, a sphere unto itself.

When the children began to arrive Asma ordered a bed made to her specifications, wide enough to hold all of them. They slept there, limbs entangled as if they had all sprouted at once from her body which lay there among them. She persuaded the artist that, once branded by childbearing, a mother's embrace could no longer be a lover's embrace. Now it was about giving milk and security to these open mouths, and waving protective scents in front of these tiny noses.

Every birth confirmed to her that this was what her life meant: hearing the sharp scream of life from a tiny body, so finely sculpted in all of its details, which had come out of hers. Time after time, until whenever her body stopped making new life. When Asma reached her forty-fifth birthday, her body had sprouted fourteen young plants, living for light and colour, in the artist's house, even if they took in that light away from the painter's remote paintbrush, poised in endless thrall to the bridles of his silent horses.

Abdallah

On the 20th of March 1986, when my father had his first heart attack, London was five years old and Salim was two. On the 26th of February 1992 he died in the Nahda Hospital. My son Muhammad was one year old and, though we didn't yet know it, he would turn out to be autistic.

I lived six years in constant terror at the thought of my father's death. But when he did die, it felt like he had already died several times. The last of his deaths gave no relief, no mercy. It did nothing to dispel my terror.

In the first weeks after his passing I could not sleep. I was too angry. Rage crept like a slow lit fuse through my blood, burning me as it burrowed deeper. Over and over, obsessively, I sketched the scene in my mind: me, standing next to his bed, where he lay covered with a white sheet, the odour of antiseptic everywhere, people coming in little groups into the white room, people taking him away and leading me to one of their little carts, no one offering me any condolences. The dead man must be buried first and before anything else could be said.

We arrive in the village and they take him inside the house. I hear Zarifa screaming. People are filling buckets of water, erecting the ritual palm-branch benches in the west courtyard and putting up screens. Someone ushers me in there with my father's body because I'm the one who should wash it, all by myself. Mayya's father, Azzan himself, hands me the water and instructs me how to rub my father's body, part by part, limb by limb. Judge Yusuf's son Abd al-Rahman helps me dry him off, perfume him, and wrap him in the shroud. People lift him into the bier and they set one corner of it on my shoulder. We march to the cemetery, west of al-Awafi. I can hear people saying *there is no God but God* in his honour and also the sceptical whisperings. Now Suwayd has dug the pit and Azzan lowers me into this grave so that I can receive my father's body and lay it properly on its right side. I take in the moist freshness of the soil down there. I climb up out of the grave so that others can make a layer of stones over the shrouded body before they pile up the earth. Finally they fix a large stone into the ground where his head would be, and everyone returns to al-Awafi.

At home to receive condolences, I'm greeted by one man and the next, and they all ask God to bless my period of mourning and make good come of it. I respond, over and over. God decides how long we live. There's coffee, lots of coffee, and then large trays of rice and meat. When darkness falls I return to the house, to my father's room, with nothing but this all-encompassing anger. Seven days of this, and then the mourning period – for visitors, anyway – is over.

Some years later, other details enter this picture. I'll see my father's belly tremble slightly under the bucket of cold water. The water will form a small pool, and this pond seeps out to trickle through all the alleys of al-Awafi. The odours of lotus and embalming fluid pervade the damp alleyways, and I will see my father's index finger lifted slightly, just enough to cause a slight swelling on the white death shroud. I'll see his hand sweep aside the stones and the soil. Only his hand remains there, outside the grave. I will see Zarifa amputate her own legs and pluck out the white hair on her head.

The Man in the Desert

The planet Saturn was directly ahead. The man standing alone in the desert was ready for it. He prepared the blend of ingredients that went into the smoke to be offered to Saturn. A little saffron, flax and some soiled wool, the brain of a cat. He had already checked carefully to make certain that the reigning sign was a changeable one, that the moon was where it should be, and that Saturn and Mars were both aligned facing the moon. As pleased as he was relieved by what he saw, the man breathed out a contented sigh as there flashed into his mind the woman's face in the darkness as she left his home. The Bride of the Falaj.

Now Saturn was at the pole of the sky, gazing toward the two lit bodies – the sun and moon – as the two fell away from each other.

He blended the saffron, flax, brain matter and fleece and burnt it until it was a proper incense, of the right density between his fingers. He put on the ritual garments for his communication with Saturn. Saturn! Saturn demanded a length of black and green silk. On the wrist he held closest to the planet he wore cast-iron armlets, bones in his hand.

The solitary man in the desert launched his fervent call. Great Sayyid, Victorious One, Crusher of All, Mighty Spirit, of Pure Mind and Broadest Understanding, Piercing of Gaze and Astuteness, Resilient King and Sultan who Vanquishes Time itself, Causer of Pain, Saturn! Cold Dry Star, Loyal Star, True in Affections, Master of Sorcery and Cunning, Angry and Powerful in Malice, Ever Able, Ever Realizing your Dark Promises, Bringer of Pain and Torment, Shaykh of Craft and Deception, Bringer of Woe on Whosoever Attempts to Thwart Him, of Misery to Whosoever Resists Him – I entreat you, Father of Fathers, Most Deserving of the fealty of your great ancestors and honourable associates, on the Truth of Your Creator and the One who gives you power, Bringer of all that is sublime and all that lies below the earth, Possessor of all: I entreat you to cut Najiya, daughter of Shaykha, from Azzan, son of Mayya, in the name of these spirits of the other world; to separate them as darkness is separated from light, and to lead them to despise each other, ever enemies, like the enmity between fire and water. I ask you, Great Father, to do nothing other than knotting Azzan's carnal desire for Najiya to make that knot – by the power of these otherworldly spirits – as hard and fast as the knotting of these rock faces and boulders.

Khawla

Now that Asma was married, Khawla was alone in the house with her mother. On rare occasions her father joined them. He never smiled.

Although her mother was not severe with her, Khawla felt dejected and irritated by the constricted life at home as the days went on, and she withdrew into herself more and more. Her single-minded fixation on her figure and her looks became an obsession. She almost went mad. She waited for Nasir with a conviction that simply would not admit any of the doubt others were trying to instil in her. She was Virginie in the tale of Paul and Virginie; Layla in the legend of her poet-lover's devotion, so obsessive he was nicknamed Majnun, the Mad One; she was the tragic Juliet. She was all the women through all the ages whose love had been eternal and true, who had sacrificed themselves out of loyalty to that love. The only passage that had meant anything, amongst the many cultural nuggets with which Asma was always trying to refine her, was the story about the souls split apart who were forever searching restlessly for completion and would find rest only when they were reunited. Khawla discovered that this idea was not in *The Dove's Necklace* after all, but in a much less famous book called *al-Zahra*. The important point, though, was that Nasir was her half-soul, and so he would inevitably come back.

Nasir came back.

True, she had to wait another five years and refuse at least ten offers of marriage before Nasir returned. But he came back to her.

At least, that's the way it looked to her. The truth was that Nasir came back having completely run out of funds in Canada. Years before, his scholarship had been suspended. He had lived on the very limited expense money that his mother had sent him secretly, plus minor jobs that he never stayed with for long. Then his mother died. He was thrown out of his latest job. He had no choice but to come back to al-Awafi, where he soon discovered that his mother had put conditions on her will. If he wanted his inheritance he was to marry Khawla. So he married Khawla, and he got the money, and two weeks after the wedding he flew back to Canada.

Before his mother's death, Nasir had settled down with a girlfriend in a little house in Montreal. Returning from his short funerary visit to Oman, he didn't see any compelling reason to tell her about his marriage. For ten years, Nasir returned to Oman once every two years to see the new child in his house and to leave Khawla pregnant again.

Khawla held on fiercely to her dream. Nasir had come back to her and she would not lose him a second time. The more patience she showed with his serial abandonment, the more estimable she seemed in her own eyes, if not in anyone else's, and the more sense it all made to her. Her painful life was exemplary; it was the epitome of the greatest sort of love, a sublime and self-immolating love that could not be shattered by anything, not even the cruel harshness of the lover, who would no sooner arrive in Oman than he would wrap himself in long telephone conversations; who hung a photo of his Canadian girlfriend on his car key ring; who brought fancy clothes from Canada for his children but never in the right sizes because he didn't even know how old they were.

Whenever her sisters or her mother rebuked her, Khawla's response was the same. He works there, but he'll come back to his own country in the end. He'll come to his senses, he'll come back to his wife and children, and his home. He's a good man at heart and that's what will bring him back.

When her dream came true – when the Canadian girlfriend left Nasir, throwing him out of the house in Montreal – he and Khawla had already been married for a decade. He came back. He found a good job in a company, and he began to get to know his wife and children.

Abdallah

At about the age of ten, London would accompany her mother regularly on jaunts to The Family Bookstore in Muscat. Her mother always bought children's books in English for her. Although by then there were quite a few bookstores in the city, The Family Bookstore was the oldest and remained the most prominent. It was no longer dedicated to the purpose for which it had been established late in the nineteenth century: founded and built as a shop specialising in Bibles, it was an arm of the American missionary effort in Oman. But at some point, someone realised that a general bookstore offering a good range of titles would be more appealing to the ordinary reader than a shop selling the Gospels. And so, in the late 1960s, it acquired a new name and a larger footprint, and there were even attempts to launch branch outlets. The reputation it gradually made for itself as a secular bookstore led to criticism. The Middle East Council of Churches invested in major efforts to return it to its missionary commitments.

Mayya wasn't concerned with the bookstore's religious history. She had a single, clear goal: that London learn to read in English. Later, her aim was that Muhammad learn to speak. When he turned five her efforts finally bore fruit and the boy began to talk. But he used words differently than other children did, and his communications with us remained fundamentally dependent on signs and gestures.

Although the doctors made it clear to me that autism was not an inherited condition, nor did it have anything to do with the environment, the uncertainty about what had caused it persuaded Mayya and me not to have any more children.

When I see Muhammad, I try to remember things about my own childhood. How did I feel about life when I was his age? But whatever floats to the surface of my consciousness is connected to the Big House, built of gypsum plaster which my father rebuilt in cement, adding on many more rooms. I can remember the exact colours of the balls I was not allowed to play with in the street with the other boys; the tiny flashing mirrors on my Indian-made coat; the statuesque figure of my uncle's wife before they moved to Wadi Aday; the fat gold bracelets on my aunt's wrist; the fragrance of the paper-thin bread as Zarifa pulled it from the hot oven; the horn of peppercorns in my mouth on the day Habib married her.

I bought her for twenty coins, my father would say. At the worst of the economic crisis, when a big sack of rice imported from Calcutta or Madras cost one hundred coins, and Zarifa cost twenty.

These were the silver Maria Theresa coins which could not be faked because the silver was so pure. My father hoarded them, keeping ten or twenty or fifty in the leather bag that he always knotted onto his belt. For a long time he had nothing but scorn for the paper riyals that had since appeared, until he was forced to bow to their superior power.

Mayya, on the other hand, seemed completely enamoured of riyals. Her dream, she told me, was that we acquire as many riyals as we possibly could so that we could leave al-Awafi and build a nice house in Muscat. Meanwhile, her mother was demanding that I promise not to take her to the city. That irritated Mayya. She would not live forever, her whole and entire life, under the sway of her mother, in the way that I lived completely cowed by my father's every word, she declared. When the rumours spread about the disappearance of the alluring Bedouin woman, her father's lover, Mayya said, My mother has something to do with this. But her mother was a woman who never left the house. How could she have played a role in the woman's disappearance?

Some said the Bedouin woman had come down with a mysterious disease that made parts of her beautiful body drop off, or that her limbs were rotting away, before she vanished. Others said she sold her house and camel and went to settle in Matrah in order to sell her Bedouin needlework. Still others said she had suddenly gone mad and so her friends carried her off to Ibn Sina Hospital. Word also went around that her neighbours, who had turned the satellite dish in their two-storey house into an enormous trough where their livestock ate clover, responded to her sarcastic words about them by training her mongoloid brother to shoot bullets and making him believe that his sister had brought shame upon all of them. They taught him how to use the pistol. They buried the corpse secretly one night beneath the biggest sand dune.

Khalid

Asma asked, Why do you draw, Khalid?

To free myself from existing only inside the narrow space of my father's imagination, and then to re-invent my life in the space of my own. All the time I was a child, and all the way into my early twenties, my father's view of me was defined by what he saw in his head. He had his own fancies and it was always very clear just how far they went – and no further. I was the fuel that fired his imagination and his whole image of me, forever, was based on his absolute certainty that I would be the living version of what was in his mind. He never questioned this! So, doing art became as necessary to me as drinking water and breathing air, and that began in the very moment I realised I couldn't live this way, I couldn't survive without following my own imagination. Art and imagination are alike in that way, Asma. They give some kind of worth to my existence. No matter how fine and pleasant reality may be, without imagination life becomes ... well, unbearable.

Do you see the way people move through life – and I mean, just the little bits of their lives you can see? Most of their movement through life is invisible, it goes on inside of them, so for us it exists beneath the surface. Their own private worlds, their imaginations. When I liberated myself from living through my father's head I created my own imagination with a paintbrush. I grew my hair long, and my beard, I wore jeans I'd ripped up deliberately, and I dropped out of the College of Engineering so I could enter the College of Fine Arts.

Sometimes I went on painting until I collapsed from exhaustion. If I was doing anything else, even just walking down the street or something simple like that, I felt like part of my hand was missing because it wasn't holding a paintbrush. The brush was part of my hand, growing with it. My brush breathed the same way I did. I lived in my paintings, whatever was outside no longer concerned me, or touched me, really. All I needed was my imagination. The energy I had for sketching and painting was insane. It was as if I was suffering from a fever: I lived in a fog of sweat and delirium and feeling completely, absolutely one with my art.

My art saved me from acting out the image my father had made for me. Issa the Emigrant couldn't forget for a moment that he was an emigrant. He carried his history like it was his destiny, and he was always working to make sure his firstborn son would carry his history too. This son of his would be his revenge, which he could wave in the face of defeat, frustration, and forced absence from the homeland that had betrayed him.

Every day, Issa the Emigrant closed his eyes to open them onto the truth of his identity. He would go out and mingle in the Cairo streets, he would spend evenings chatting with Egyptians, he put his children through Egyptian universities. But he didn't forget for a second that he was Issa, son of Shaykh Ali, who carried the burden and the woes of Oman on his shoulders. Shaykh Ali was in the delegation that accompanied Shaykh Issa bin Salih, the Imam's ambassador, on the day the famous Treaty of Sib was signed between the

English and the Sultan, on one side, and the Imam and the tribes allied with him on the other. He never forgot how positively overjoyed his father was when this treaty was signed. It gave them freedom of movement in the interior, and influence on more tribes, and helped them spread their calls for unity and organization in preparation to go against the English. All the details of his history and identity kept Issa the Emigrant awake nights. Many times he made me listen to him talk about the spirits of his grandfathers that he believed he was now faithfully representing on earth. His great-grandfather Shaykh Mansur bin Nasir was among the cavalry who combated Mutlaq the Wahhabi in his repeated raids on Omanis. He was in the battle where the Omanis held on so fiercely to their swords that their hands were stiff and rigid around them by the time darkness fell. In their songs the women recount how women soaked the fighters' hands in water until they softened enough for the swords to drop. Shaykh Mansur's name itself was in more than one of those women's songs, which they went on singing in their wedding parties long after the event. Songs that expressed the extraordinary courage of the shaykh whose white steed flew with him, his hands firm on his sword, putting terror in the men of Mutlaq al-Wahhabi. Issa the Emigrant carried on his back the souls of those forefathers. He fought at Jabal al-Akhdar at the side of the Imam Ghalib al-Hina'i. He buried their martyrs with his own hands and carried secret missives under cover of darkness. When they were defeated and scattered he fled. He emigrated, but it was only his body that went. His soul was too heavy to go.

What did he want to make me into? A fighter? A martyr? A young shaykh feeding the hungry and finding refuge for the weak? A shaykh of today who would stamp his approval on letters containing the demands of Bedouins and peasants? Some kind of opposition activist? What? When the revolution took fire in Dhofar he refused to even discuss it. He simply rejected the whole idea, and he was furious about the whole thing. Those Communists? he would shout. Out of the question! This will never suit Oman. Never.

Every evening, I had to read passages from the book *The Gem of Notable People in the History of the Folk of Oman* by Shaykh al-Salmi out to him until I had the whole text by heart. He used to take me with him to the Nile River Corniche in the late afternoons and while we were walking he would ask me to recite the famous poem by Abu Muslim al-Bahlani, with its powerful memories of his early life. To recite it from the first line all the way to end. He explained to me – many times he explained to me! – that this nineteenth-century fellow, Abu Muslim, might be an Omani but he was no less a poet than was his famous Egyptian contemporary Ahmad Shawqi. You really must learn by heart every last poem he composed, he would exclaim. And not only the poem that everyone knows. But how he cried when I recited lines from it.

Stabs of lightning pierce me like the wail of the grieved cameleer
Why, sad one, are you somnolent and dull?
Its grim swords clove the heavens, in an army of clouds to rush onward
O homeland sorely missed, clouds and rain over all.

And then when I got to certain other lines he made me repeat them tens of times.

Those places in which I could not stay on and on
Yet in my hope-filled mind, still they reside
Far away have I gone but never have I left them:
But then, how many times is body torn from soul!

Then he would take over, reciting the next section of the poem himself, but only getting so far, always as far as the same line.

I departed them, overruled, and I could not prevail
No person can surmount what is decreed

With a heavy sigh, almost a moan, he would ask me to go on while he listened without another word. He was completely infatuated with Abu Muslim al-Bahlani and he told me all about the man. He was so many things: a reformer, a man of enlightenment, and it seems he had some kind of intuitive creativity. Early in the century, Abu Muslim founded the first Omani newspaper. He called it *Success* and published it from Zanzibar, where he was living then. And his poetry collection was the first volume of verse by an Omani ever published. He wrote many other books, like, on Islamic jurisprudence, and on morals. My father was always keen to get his hands on first editions of whatever Abu Muslim wrote. Abu Muslim supported the Imams and scholars in Oman heart and soul, even though fate never allowed him to meet most of them. My father handled his affairs while he was in exile. He worked closely with some other supporters to print al-Bahlani's poetry along with some other Omani books at the Aleppo Press in Cairo. We spent long hours stacking up the copies, organising them so customers could see them, but I have no idea, and I didn't then, how my father planned to market them, or even distribute them. Who would read them, anyway?

My father enrolled me in the College of Engineering because, he said, the future in Oman was for engineers and lawyers. And time after time he hinted – very clearly! – that if I knew what was good for me I wouldn't so much as glance at any Egyptian girl. In fact, he put it to me bluntly. We may live here but we're not from here. We won't leave anything of ourselves here. When we die our coffins will be carried to Oman. That's where we'll be buried.

This kept me awake at night – the attempt to imagine this place, which I barely had any childhood memories of, since I had been made to leave it so early. What particularly tormented me was the image of our coffins, black and gloomy, lined up next to each other. My father's coffin, my mother's, mine, my sister's, my brother's coffin – lying in the hold of an airplane taking off for the impossible journey that we would never make while alive, the journey from Cairo to Muscat. And the image of us as dead, us, lifted out of our boxes by relatives I would never have gotten to know, so we could be buried in her shrouds under the burning sun west of al-Awafi, in the graveyard where not a single tree grew, not even any scrubby little desert bushes. So many times I hoped my father would reverse his plan, that he would have us buried in one of Cairo's cemeteries, so noisy with movement and life, with their vendors and Qur'an reciters – or that he would put us in an airplane, live bodies rather than corpses, headed for Muscat. That he wouldn't already assign our coffins to the hold.

When I could finally shake myself loose, when I managed to no longer live inside the image of me he had in his head, I finally found out what freedom tastes like. It was such a good taste! People choose their own books, ones they actually want to read. And their own friends, and the cities they're fond of. How liberated a person feels when it's finally no longer a question of being just an extension or embodiment of someone else's fancy, even if that someone else is your father. My chronic headaches ended and I lost my pathological fear of being inside a closed-in dark place. Suddenly I was addicted to spending all my hours in the streets of Cairo, my streets, I had not known any others – and with real friends, ones who yelled out slogans as they marched in the streets, who drew pictures and had dreams and could tease each other. People who weren't simply the faded mental creations of their families or their elders, and whose blurred identities or boundaries made them seem more like ethereal angels whom I couldn't actually see or touch. Issa the Emigrant went quiet. He didn't come to my first exhibition, he didn't read a single article on my art and he treated me with a coldness that was probably both disdain and despair. But just when I began to forget that there existed a place called Oman, my sister Ghaliya died.

I hadn't ever had the feeling that our worlds were so linked, so frighteningly enmeshed, the worlds of me and my family, until Ghaliya died. Our worlds fell apart. We all found the world we inhabited collapsed around us, My father and mother, me, my brother. In front of the simple question of where to bury her, it suddenly became frighteningly clear to me – to me, the free, the liberated, artist – whose head was full of freedom – how deep the hidden ties between us went, how strong they were, and how my world could be destroyed in a moment if theirs caved in.

I think it was only two days before my father's hair turned white! We packed our cases. We returned, all of us, still alive. Not Ghaliya though. She was a shadow of my nightmarish imagination. In her coffin in the hold.

No longer was the voyage to Oman an impossible trip. It wasn't just a round-trip ticket, either, a little space in which we would bury a beloved sister, and return in all simplicity to Cairo, to our home, our work, our friends. No. This unexpected trip itself bonded us in some hidden but really profound way. The trip was the strong rope that tied us together and would yank us out of the dream and the nightmare both, at the same time. It freed us from the idea that returning was impossible or unreal. It made returning into something you could actually do, something likely, and – we suspected it then – permanent, too. Ghaliya paid for our liberation with her death. There had to be an offering, a sacrifice. A bridge across which my father walked, and we followed, to Oman. Ghaliya's dead body, her coffin, which was carried to the treeless cemetery in al-Awafi – the coffin of the daughter born in Cairo, the daughter who lived in Cairo – was our bridge.

Asma and the moon

Asma, still a bride, came to visit her father. Not long after her wedding he had suddenly come down with a fever no one could diagnose, and he was bedridden. His temperature wouldn't come down. When Azzan saw her he leaned back against a cushion and asked her to recite some of al-Mutanabbi's poetry. Asma's voice was subdued at first but it started gathering fervour as she recited.

With the sedan-chairs' departure my nights are long
For lovers' nights stretch endless
They show me the full moon I have no craving for
And hide a moon to which there is no way
After the loved ones, I have not lived in solace
But ahh, the misfortunes—those still must I bear

Her father's hand went up and Asma stopped. Staring at his hands, she noticed how pale and weak they looked, and how white the hair was at the roots, where it was parted. She felt confused. The room seemed very hot, radiating his fever. She was embarrassed at the traces of henna still visible on her hands. She wished she had the courage to use her hands, to press them against her father's robe, to make him lie flat on his bed and then to smooth his hair. The air was so heavy. She had an odd urge to apologise to him but she didn't know why.

The lotus-thorn tree had grown enough that its leaves now pressed against the window. The heat seemed to be getting worse. A vision of her future children crowding into the room to surround their grandfather's bed forced itself on her but the image seemed to erase his pale face. She was confused into complete silence but his hand rescued her. His fingers were trying to grasp a barely visible tattered notebook tightly enough to tug it out from under his pillow. Asma studied the title: *From the Sessions of the Brilliant Scholar Judge Yusuf bin Abd al-Rahman*. When she cracked open the bound notebook, its pages fell open where a leaf had been stuck as a bookmark. Azzan nodded at her. She began to read.

Know that the stars of the firmament empty their gems into the moon, and the moon spills them into the water. The force of the water splits them into all the gems that exist in creation. The moon is the treasure house for what is on high and what lies below. The moon moves between high and low, between the sublime and the filth of creation. Of all the celestial bodies, the moon is closest to the matters of this lower world. And so it is a guide to all things. Contemplate the state of the moon until you know it well. Its soundness is the strength of all things, its ruin the corruption of all things. If the moon moves closer to another celestial body then it gives more force to whatever that body can tell us or give us. When the moon moves away from another body in the firmament it weakens that sphere's power. When the moon's light intensifies in its approach to Mercury, that is the best state of all. But if the moonlight is weak as it confronts Saturn, or moves closer to it, this is the worst of all worlds.

Abdallah's mother

A woman as young and as strong as Fatima Umm Abdallah could not possibly die in a matter of two or three days unless she'd contracted a fever as she was giving birth. That's what people in al-Awafi said. Ankabuta made certain that everyone knew she had carried the special childbirth food regularly to the jinn-woman Baqiia so that the jinni would not harm Fatima, or baby Abdallah. And Ankabuta swore that she hadn't taken even one bite from the huge tray of food she carried on her head to Baqiia. She always left the food, exactly as she had brought it, at the jinn-woman's favourite rock. And then she left immediately without even once looking behind her. Not long before this, Zayd claimed, the young woman whose death was so puzzling had uprooted the basil bush herself rather than summoning him to do it. And that she told him the odour of basil attracts vipers and she was afraid for Abdallah. Even if he was a newborn, it wouldn't be that long before he could sit up, and then soon after that he would be crawling.

Merchant Sulayman's sister insisted that she had been very careful. She had supervised the food preparation herself. But somehow, within days, the poor woman changed colour. She turned blue. Zayd insisted she was the sort of woman who simply couldn't escape being the target of someone's sorcery. He was very sure of what he was saying, he told them, especially since he was the one who worked all night long at the canals outside town, and so he knew all the secrets of the night-folk. She was a good woman who minded her own business, Maneen said sadly, and she didn't forget to send him sweets after the boy was born.

Shaykh Said's mother said that every person in this world will be served in the afterlife what she served others in this life. God forbears. He does not neglect the good ones among us, she said.

People were startled by her words. What was she hinting at?

Zarifa kept quiet.

Cousin Marwan

Even when he was very little, Marwan remembers, he had heard his mother tell the story of the dream she'd had when she was pregnant with him, and Judge Yusuf's interpretation. You will have a son, he said, who will be righteous and good. Pure, and an important man. She wanted to name him Muhammad or Ahmad, but the baby already had brothers with these names. So she named him Marwan, seeking a good omen from the name of her deceased brother who had raised her. She brought the boy up on the soundness of her dream, which she believed in fiercely, and that's why she gave him a second moniker, 'the Pure', which everyone else began to use, too. She worked hard to implant a love of knowledge and devotion to the Faith in him from his early days, and she pushed him toward the Shaykh at the mosque, wanting Marwan to shadow him. That's the way he grew up, his heart attached to the mosque.

Marwan the Pure committed to heart the whole of the Noble Hadith. Surely this alone was proof that he was amongst the elect, those whom God would shade and protect on the Day when there is no shade to be had but His. Marwan grew up obeying God to the letter. Because his heart was so attached to the mosque he scorned the games of other boys and their interest in trivial things. He found nothing to admire about the time people spent in wasteful pleasures. He had no use for chitchat or for anything else that stole moments from the quiet contemplation of God's creation. He buried himself in this pure little world that encased him. When his parents moved to Wadi Aday, leaving al-Awafi, they chose a house near the mosque so that their children would be raised on the threshold of the mosque there, and particularly so that, in the new environment, Marwan the Pure would not find himself cut off from his life of devotions.

He was number four, following Hamad, Muhammad and Qasim. After him came Hilal and Asim. But he himself recognised early that he was made of a different clay, and he was acutely aware of the pride his parents took in him. He knew how they talked about him. He stayed apart, refusing to play with his brothers or even exchange much conversation with them. These silly matters were not worthy of him, whose specialness had been foretold in the dream, who was vowed and destined to works of greatness.

Marwan the Pure was thirteen when he snuck in the night to his parents' room and stole all the money he found in his father's wallet. The next day he beat himself sore with his father's cane and vowed to fast for two weeks. Three months later he snuck into his big brothers' room and stole the money in Qasim's wallet.

By the time Marwan had completed his sixteenth year, he had fasted a total of eight months and fourteen days as penance for his thefts. The neighbours swore that light poured from his face and that his eyes, fasting from the fleeting pleasures of this world, gave off the everlasting grace of the hereafter. The girls were crazy in love with his slow, leisured, gentle gait, the pace of a person who has nothing to fear. They adored his grave eyes that never met the gaze of any girl. No one saw the traces of the self-inflicted blows to his back, punishment for all he had stolen, which by now consisted not only of money but also included watches and articles of clothing, even his mother's earrings and shoes. More often, now, he dressed only in white, and he rarely spoke. And when his face went pale from so much fasting, no one remained in doubt that he was some kind of saint, one of the pious, righteous Friends of God.

Yes, by the time Marwan reached the end of his sixteenth year, he had fasted a total of eight months and fourteen days but he knew very well that he would not stop stealing, just as he was perfectly aware that he had no need of any of the things he stole. He hadn't come to terms with the shock his own behaviour gave to his pure nature. What could he think? He didn't believe this creature was really him, the boy who spent so much time in devotions at the mosque, who crept into rooms at night and stole worthless objects. It ripped him apart; he could almost hear the sounds of his body splitting and shredding. Everything got confused, his mother's dream and his own grand sense of himself, trivial games and pleasures. And he stole, he whom God Himself was to screen with the formidable shade of His heavenly throne. He stole. The Pure One who was ever watchful to keep himself clean, who barely raised his eyes from the ground. He stole. The one who had been vowed to God, the one of whom glad tidings had come. He stole. His pure hands reached to steal that which he did not even need and would certainly never use.

Marwan the Pure did not reveal his secret. He scorned himself to the measure that others esteemed his worth. He despised others to the measure that he valued himself. He deafened his ears to the sound of the tearing that echoed so loudly inside him but that no one else could hear. The closed circle of his life tightened around him. He dedicated himself to fasting and isolation and worship as his heart fractured in agonizing pain.

Marwan did not reveal his secret to anyone. He did not dare, in his aloneness and apartness, to extend his hands to his Lord, in hopes that He might show him the way. For Marwan was certain that he knew the right path: this was the only one. He was the Pure One and he must remain thus, as people had come to know him, as his mother had willed him to be, as he himself had been convinced of. This thieving hand of his – he would amputate it if it returned to its ways.

After his father died and his mother came out of her mourning period, he snuck into her room one night and stole her new perfume, his father's silver dagger, and a paltry sum of money he found on the table. Moments before dawn he cut the veins in his thieving hand with the sharp dagger blade. Ever pure, ever alone, Marwan bled to death.

Sulayman

In the 1890s a major slump in the Omani date trade drove a young merchant by the name of Hilal to seek a new source of profit that would let him benefit from all the mercantile experience he'd already accumulated. Resourceful Hilal realised quickly that the arms trade was the smart alternative. Sultan Faisal's 1891 proclamation instructed Omanis to refrain from importing weapons into Jawadir Port, but Merchant Hilal and his commerce-savvy friends became increasingly dependent on weapons as a sure source of profit, especially since they could channel guns to the Afghans who seemed to need a constant supply for their raids and their feuds. Loads of smuggled weapons came in from Persian merchants on the coast, to be stored in clandestine warehouses until they could be sold to men coming from the tribes of Baluchistan and Afghanistan. Some merchants succeeded in smuggling weapons all the way to India and Zanzibar, but Merchant Hilal preferred dealing with the Afghans and Persians, since he believed that the port of Jawadir was a safer bet than any of the other possibilities. But Hilal found his commerce badly reversed after taxes were raised on weapons imports. Never mind, though – the trade revived with the new century, and Hilal joined forces with a group of Indian merchants who were importing guns directly from Europe. They were led by a man called Kemji Ram Das. On the 22nd of January 1908, when the S.S. Jayuladala arrived in the port of Muscat coming from Europe, Merchant Hilal's share was fifty full chests of ammunition. He'd already managed to sell popcorn rifles in Jawadir port for seventy dollars each and that made him a rich man very quickly. Now he sought marriage into a shaykhly family in al-Awafi. His son and heir, Sulayman, was born after more than ten years of marriage.

Nevertheless, his son's arrival must be a good omen, thought Merchant Hilal. A good start to founding a dynasty. Siblings would surely arrive. But every boy born to Hilal after Sulayman was kidnapped by death while still a nursing baby. People whispered that Sulayman was afflicted with *qashi'a*, and the disease must be fatal to his little brothers. His father took him to a specialist who sat the little boy in front of him and peered into his skull to find the errant vein in his head that – if it flared and moved too far – would mean the death of every boy born after him. When the doctor pinpointed the location of the vein, he shouted the news at the top of his voice. He heated a metal skewer over a flame and seared Sulayman's head where he believed the vein – or the qashi'a – to be, until it died completely, never making another appearance that would kill his male siblings. So Merchant Hilal had three children who lived: Sulayman and his very last son Ishaq.

There was also a girl, scrawny and pale, who spent her entire childhood as a recluse, mind and body shut away, until she was married off to a maternal cousin, and later on, to that cousin's brother. Both cousins divorced her in turn. Zarifa hated her.

Ishaq resembled his mother in her hesitant bearing and introversion. It was Sulayman who inherited everything: his father's mercantile savvy, quick mind, tall and imposing figure, grave dignity, and the large house built of plaster – as well as his nervous disposition and the title of Merchant. But Sulayman did not trade in weapons. To all appearances, dates were what occupied his work days, although his real profits were built on the slave trade.

Masouda, still here

In her shut-away room that had once been a threshing floor, Masouda realised that her daughter Shanna had gone away with her husband, Sanjar. She knew she would not see her daughter again, and that now, her food and hygiene were hostage to the charity of the neighbour women.

Day by day her voice grew fainter as she repeated, I am here...over here. I am Masouda. Her frame was more bent than ever. In odd moments neighbours asked themselves if Masouda would be buried in her misshapen posture or whether, after death, her spine would regain its straightness.

Memories of the distant past, as cloudy as they were, began to fill Masouda's head as the days she was living through and those just before grew ever more absent. She began to see moments in time that, years ago, she had not believed her head would ever be capable of facing.

She saw a thick dark dawn and herself going to gather wood. She heard a rustling in the room of Merchant Sulayman. She could not control her natural curiosity. She pressed herself to the wall and peered into the back window.

He and his wife had been sleeping in separate rooms since the birth of his son Abdallah three weeks before, so he was alone when his sister rapped on the door and immediately, without hearing a response, opened it and came in. He turned in his bed. Everything all right? he asked, startled.

She stared at him. Your wife, she said.

He got out of bed, took his dishdasha from the iron hook and struggled into it. He faced his sister. What about my wife? What's wrong? You're the one who said to me, Get married, stop doing your business with the slave women. So I married this woman. Then you carped at me, Why haven't you had a baby yet? And she's had this boy. What do you want now?

He was sitting on the edge of the bed. She stood over him. Her voice, always low, was quiet now, but he heard her. I saw her, she said. Her and Saleem, Shaykh Said's slave. At the basil bush.

Merchant Sulayman began to shiver. She finished what she had to say without any change in the tone of her voice: Never mind, leave it all to me. And she went out.

That morning, Merchant Sulayman had to travel to Salalah for some business. When he returned three months later, his wife had died, leaving tiny Abdallah in the care of his paternal aunt. Saleem, Shaykh Said's slave, had vanished.

Masouda thought she had obliterated this murky dawn scene from her mind.

Abdallah

I am not sitting in this seat suspended between heaven and earth waiting to arrive in Frankfurt any moment now. I am in Zarifa's lap in the east courtyard of the Big House, my eyes open to the full moon high in the sky, Zarifa is stroking my hair and telling me a story.

Every day when Mama Goat left the house, she warned her oldest children, Zayd and Rabab, saying, If anyone knocks, do not open the door. It could be Mr Wolf and he would eat you up. If it's me at the door, I will say, Yoo Rabab, yoo Zayd, open the door! On your mama's back there's grass to eat, and good good milk in each teat! When you hear me say that, you can open the door. So the children obeyed her. But one day Mr Wolf heard Mama Goat reminding her children what to do. After she'd gone, he began rapping on the door, and saying, Yoo Rabab, yoo Zayd, open the door! On your mama's back there's grass to eat, and good good milk in each teat! He'd changed his voice and he fooled the children. They opened the door and Mr Wolf ate them up.

When Mama Goat came home she began knocking at the door. She knocked and knocked, but in vain, as she repeated her words. Yoo Rabab, yoo Zayd ... When she'd gotten no answer she butted the door open with her horns and went inside. But she didn't find Zayd or Rabab.

Mama Goat went outside at a run to search for her little ones. She passed a spider, she passed a lamb. She asked everyone she passed, Did you see my children? But they all said, No, they hadn't seen them. Until she passed a dove. The wolf came by here, said the dove. And his stomach was very big. He must have eaten your children. Quick, go after him, you will find him asleep under the rocks. First, Mama Goat hurried to the blacksmith. She asked him to sharpen her horns until they were knife blades. She found the wolf asleep. She drove her horns into him and sliced his tummy wide open. Her children came out, and she said, Come, come! And Mama and babies all went home.

London

The minute she puts down the phone, London will jump out of bed, scattering her teddy bears – a rose-coloured streak here and a red one there. Picking up her phone again, she will call her friend Hanan. She has to tell her everything Ahmad has said, as she paces round and round her room.

Bismillahi al-rahman al-rahim, girl! Do you know what time it is?

Listen, Hanan, the new poem he's going to recite in the Oman Poetry Festival, which is coming up – it is dedicated to me!

So what? Hanan replies in English.

So what? Don't you see? I am his inspiration, his angel, his muse! I'm the beautiful demon of his poetry, as the Arab poets all used to say.

Well, congratulations to you, my dear. Can I go back to sleep now, seeing as I don't really understand poetry at all, and I only believe in well-tested scientific analyses that give guaranteed results?

On the day they concluded their betrothal vows and the marriage contract was signed, the minute they said goodbye and he left her father's home, it was almost time for the dawn prayers. She called her friend.

Hanan! I am the *most blissful* girl in the whole wide world!

A thousand congratulations, love, you certainly deserve it. So is your little dove-love time together done?

He's just left.

Did he kiss you?

No, Hanan! He told me our marriage is a victory over the disgusting hidebound class structure of society, and a crowning of true love.

She heard a laugh. You mean, he gave you a lecture instead of making the most of his opportunity? I mean, this was the contract, right? Couldn't he at least kiss you?

Hanaaan, stop it.

Hanan's frankness no longer smarted; London was too used to it. Anyway, Hanan's position on all of this had been clear from the start. Ahmad? You mean, the guy who calls himself a poet? Who is with someone new every day? Even his poetry is too heavy for anyone to bear. Why would you want him? Even his appearance . . . like, he doesn't even know what to do, sometimes he lets his beard go and other times he shaves and either way he looks wrong. One day you see him in a dishdasha, the next in jeans. Monday his hair is long and Tuesday his skull is shaved. He'll be acting like the most religious of the religious, and then the next time you see him, he's cocking around like he's the latest thing.

Ahmad had put a lot of effort into securing London. You are the girl of my dreams, he would say. He pursued her with emails and phone calls and real letters on paper, with poems and songs and photos. She was hooked.

When her mother discovered the business, she locked London up in her room and smashed her phone. The more London resisted, the more stubborn her mother became, as if she wanted to see how far her daughter would go. How hard would she hold onto this dream of hers? Or it was like

Mayya was punishing herself, and not her daughter at all, not the woman in love.

London's father was bewildered and torn. When he finally cracked the whip, decreeing she could have this marriage, her mother simply withdrew.

On the day the contract was signed, after all of the guests had gone, Ahmad kissed her hands. Do you know what it is about you that attracted me, London? That you're a girl who isn't easy. And when you did decide to love me back, you loved sincerely, and you defended your love in the face of all this backwardness and ugliness that surrounds us on every side.

Ever since she had met him she had heard him repeat these two words. Backwardness. Ugliness. Sometimes he added 'abhorrent classism'. When she saw him laughing with the woman who headed the students' literary collective, as he clasped both of her hands, he did show a bit of embarrassment. They went out to her car. He defended himself but it was more like an attack, even though she hadn't started it. Listen to me, London. Yes, you are my fiancée. My beloved. But don't start hemming me in with your jealousy and egotism and possessiveness and reaction, okay? This selfishness is ugly, and jealousy is backward, and possessiveness is one of the primitive practices from the times of hateful classism. I am a poet. A man of letters. My soul is free, completely free, like a dove in the sky. Ah, yes, my words remind me of Mahmoud Darwish's poem – the dove flies, the dove lands … Anything that ties me down throttles me. Stifles my creativity. Kills my rush of poetic language. I want a woman who understands me. A woman who knows perfectly well that I am the wind and she is the tree. She sends her roots into the ground, I circle overhead in the sky.

London didn't say anything, not then. She tugged her lab coat tightly around her, ate the falafel sandwich he had bought her from Café Nasir, and realised that he'd given her a clear view of his chin, which she didn't usually see like this because he didn't usually carry his face tipped so high. This time, trying to stare him in the eye all she could see was his chin, bobbing up and down with his words and the sandwich he was eating.

Some weeks later she discovered a photograph of the president of the literary collective in his wallet. She was so angry that she tore it to shreds immediately. Ahmad shouted at her. You silly woman, this photo is just some of the material for the booklet we're doing for the poetry event. What a stupid thing to do. Backward, and ugly!

They stopped speaking.

London needed someone to talk to. But she didn't want to expose herself to Hanan's irritation and sarcasm. She knew Hanan's opinion well enough. I warned you, Hanan would snap at her. Every new poem is dedicated to a new girl. Why did you allow him to insult you like that?

Hanan didn't understand. London was certain he loved her, and that he was telling her the truth. What business did she have with his previous life? It didn't concern her a bit. The important thing was their future together, and she didn't want to fail. She was afraid of failure, it terrified her. It was three o'clock in the morning and she called him.

The next day they went in his car with the darkened windows for a long drive on the shore. He rejected her suggestion that they get out and walk, because it was so hot. They ate ice cream and talked about the future. As soon as I finish my intern year I'll open a private clinic, and then after you graduate you can join it. Your father will help us start it. Once I've got more famous for my poetry, I'll leave the whole thing to you so I can free myself up to follow my talent. You'll be the wife of the greatest poet of Oman! For that matter, the most celebrated poet in the whole Arab world. In the darkness of the car, he embraced her.

London's dream was somewhat different. After finishing her intern year she would work in the government's hospitals long enough to get experience. Then she would travel to Canada for a further degree in paediatric medicine. After that she might consider the clinic idea. But she couldn't discuss any of this. The smell of his shampoo filled her nose and she gave in to his hugs. She imagined what their children would look like and she put her arms around him. London wasn't blind. She did see all the signs, but she wouldn't let her mind accept them.

Look here, Hanan said. This romance thing. With all due respect for love wherever it is, to lovers, songs, Nizar Qabbani's poetry, flowers, the moon, nights of conversation, stars, and every poet who has ever existed – this isn't big on rationality. No listening, no looking, no thinking or real planning. A guy you saw a few times in lecture halls and at poetry evenings and you talked to him in the hall for a few minutes and then on the phone a few nights. You split a sandwich in the hospital cafeteria on your break and you drank a Pepsi together in the med college parking lot. And then you say, I'm crazy about him? I can't live without him? He is my air and water, my sun and moon? What's this nonsense? And it turns out his grandfather was a shepherd for your grandmother's father fifty years ago and your grandmother swears she'll slit your throat if you marry him? They hit you and break your phone and forbid you going to classes for several days, and why? For some guy who is no different than thousands of other men in this world? He's not even as tall as you are. And you say to me 'love' and patience and sacrifice and if I don't marry him I will kill myself? If I can't talk to him I can't breathe and if I don't see him I can't live? What love, London? Did you, like, walk into him deliberately so you could fall in love, in the first place? You're always saying to me, it's the phone calls, the emails… well, this is exactly your mistake, London. When you are not truly with someone, and you only hear his voice, and then all he talks about is himself, you form the image that you're already hoping for. You don't exactly get a true picture. See, you don't know him at all. Poetry and dreamy phone conversations wa *salam!* That's all you've got! And then – either I marry him or I kill myself? And I'm so great because I'm rejecting the hateful class system? You don't need his slogans in order to trust your own principles, London. What has he done for your sake anyway? He lets your mother torture you and your grandmother threaten you, and all he does is just sit there watching, waiting to see what the outcome will be. This is a man? This guy? As far as I'm concerned what marriage is doesn't have a lot to do with love. Love is dreams, marriage is for real: life, responsibility, child-ren. No illusions. The right person is the one who respects and honours you, and you feel totally comfortable with, the one who will be a father you can be proud of, for your children's sake. Not someone with a stupid inferiority complex who makes you feel jealous. Love, he said. Hah! I swear I thought you had some brains, London. I thought your mind was on graduating, and on Canada, your specialization – until all of this happened. What are you going to do now, if your mother keeps on slapping you, if they don't marry you to him?

I *will* kill myself.

Hanan left. She was assigned to a school in Dhofar. Refusing was out of the question. If she turned this job down she'd lose her chances, probably forever. Where would she find a fixer who could get her appointed in Muscat so that she could stay with her family? She didn't know anyone with any influence, and if she said no and the job flew out of her hands all the dreams of her family would go up in smoke – her father, retired now, her mother, who was ill, her brother who had gotten engaged seven years before but on his miserable salary had still not been able to pay the dowry. She packed her cases and travelled south, dreaming of her first salary and her brother's wedding.

London began phoning her every other day, in tears.

Hanan, I hate the words freedom and culture and classism. I've started doubting myself completely. Can you imagine, he searches my phone every time we meet, he goes through all the numbers on it to make sure there is no new one that he doesn't know.

Hanan sighed. I don't know what to say to you, love. This man doesn't deserve you.

I don't understand anything any more. It's as if I'm living inside a tornado. Suddenly he started noticing how dark and thin I am, as if he never saw me before.

I swear that guy has no shame. Why don't you stand up to him? *Talk* to him about all of this.

I've tried, and every time I start, he says to me, Don't think you are better than me. I'm the man here, and your family and all the real estate your father owns and his business don't concern me a bit. Even though, Hanan, I never said anything about my family to him. Not even once, not at all.

Allah Allah! This man is sick, sweetheart. Give it some thought before you get any deeper into it . . . you're still just in the contract period, meaning, it's just an engagement, really.

You want us to break up, Hanan? Ahmad is my darling, the dream of my life. We have to solve our problems, I don't want my first love to fail. I don't want the way I've resisted my family to go in vain. I want to prove our success to the world, to my mother and father and grandmother and our classmates, the whole world. I don't want to be a divorced woman.

But her first love did fail. It had failed long before she could admit it, and after a lot of insults and pains. Finally she demanded an annulment and refused to see him. He stood at her car door in the College parking lot and begged her to speak to him. He blocked the car door with his body to prevent her from getting in. London, my London, don't leave me . . . you are mine. You are the girl of my dreams. I swear to God I am sorry. I didn't mean to hit you. I was just angry, I swear to God, I'm so sorry, forgive me. I kiss your feet. I didn't mean what I said. I don't want to lose you, and anyway, you are my property, my London. You are my victory and my inspiration. You are mine. You would leave me and belong to someone else? wAllahi it won't happen, you belong to me. You are my girl, my wife. I kiss your hands, don't leave me. We'll get married, the date's been set and we'll go on honeymoon to Europe. We'll open the clinic together. Have you forgotten our dreams, London? You're mine, my London, my muse. My love, mine. You belong to me.

London left the parking lot and went back into the College. It wasn't enough to keep on saying to herself, I am not your possession, and I do not belong to anyone. It wasn't enough, any of this, to heal her. She knew you couldn't treat a wound just by cleansing it with an antiseptic or pretending it was only a scratch.

The desperate longing in his face and voice as they'd been before was a weapon her heart waved in her face. I hate you, I hate your voice, I hate the look of you. She tore up all the pictures of him she could find. But she couldn't feel the kind of hatred that might pull her out of this. She just felt the sharpest, most violent bitterness and pain.

Khawla

After Nasir had truly settled down in Oman, and once Khawla's two last children had arrived, and now that Nasir was hardly ever leaving the house except when he had to go to work, she decided. She wanted a divorce.

Everyone thought she had gone insane. Or perhaps she was concealing some terrible set of secrets that had pushed her to this crazy decision.

But Khawla wasn't hiding anything.

It was just that she couldn't bear the past. Everything was calm and well-ordered now. Fayiz, the youngest of her five children, was in high school. Mona was engaged to a respectable engineer, and the others were all doing well. Everything in her life was so calm, in fact, that it was like existing in a still and soundless landscape. All of it: her married life, her motherhood, her friendships.

She was at peace, so her heart stopped forgiving. She couldn't bear the past any longer. All of it seemed now to have grown to an enormous size inside her, and it choked her. Every night, the portrait of the Canadian girl on the key ring got bigger, and went to sleep on Khawla's pillow. Every day, all of those hours she had spent alone in maternity wards marched out in force to pounce on her. Every day, she could see the clothes her children never wore because their father didn't even know how old they were. Every day, she saw the years that had passed with her bed cold, her beauty wrecked, the neighbours taking her children to the hospital if they fell ill, her sisters loaning her money when she needed it, her mother scolding her, and neighbours' eyes full of pity. The past came back every single day, a warrior's lance that stabbed her through. Oh, Khawla! That wild forest inside of you, full of rough underbrush. Had it been asleep all these years, and was it you who closed its eyes? Who covered over its poisoned plants? You can see it now, though, as it rips through the old sheets with which you tried to cover it and choke off all those thorns. What does it want? You don't know, of course. How would you know? As you take a step on the staircase that leads down into it, the step before it splinters and the way back is gone. The white sheets that covered it are gone.

What she saw now was not Nasir's sweetness, the gentleness he could show, the way he did lose himself serving her and the children. She couldn't see his loyalty, his perfect respect. She saw the birthing rooms, empty except for her moaning and the newborn. She saw the long mornings of pregnancy, as she lay there sick and cold. She heard the ringing of his telephone after midnight. She heard his whisperings and his sighs into the phone, she heard the screech of airplanes lifting off the runway, heading for Canada, year after year for an entire decade, never stopping. She heard the children's screams, the clatter they made, and she felt the coldness of her bed creeping into her body. All of it, Khawla carried on her back, and the load grew heavier every day, and her back began to break.

Trying every possible argument, he begged her to take back her decision, but her ears were stopped up now. She no longer even heard his voice. She hadn't heard his voice for a long time, in fact. He pleaded with her. Words that undoubtedly would have once melted her ricocheted against her eardrums like rusty bits of iron. The fault wasn't in the words but in the years. In all those winter nights and summer days. The years dragged all of those words behind them and when the words tried to take root on her burdened back, the stony ground there threw them off. Or she ate them to the bone, the way some creatures consume their young. The years were live creatures. Khawla did not forget anything she had gone through, day by day, hour by hour, minute by minute, everything inside her sapping her spirit. Every day plunged another blade into the deep earth inside of her, turning it over mercilessly, sowing it. At the lowest point, at Khawla's bedrock, there was no fresh soil fit for planting.

There were words she wanted to say to him. Anything at all, that would have been enough for me, anything that would have watered the fields of my heart and made them flower. Anything to fill those baskets held out to you. Only to you. Anything. A letter. Just a single page with one single word, in your handwriting. The ring of a telephone after midnight, a snatched dream in which you didn't turn your back, a small step, a single slow turn to face me. Anything. Even an angry scolding! A sigh of exasperation. A cheap gift. Anything would have been a lot. But that anything never came. Nothing, ever. And now, *everything* is not enough. Everything is a lot less than a single bud, a single leaf unfolding in a field whipped by winter.

But she didn't say any of it. How to say it, to a man who had spent the last ten years working himself hard to serve his home and children, how could he understand that the seed planted in those first ten years had suddenly erupted in her body, growing thorns that tore her into shreds?

Abdallah

We were on the shore at Sib. My Lexus was parked at one of the new lamp posts that vaguely resemble the Burj al-Arab in Dubai.

Muhammad was sitting next to me. He said she was being insanely jealous, and preventing him from doing what he loved. She was spying on him, looking at his phone. The car seemed to lean into the lamp post. Who? I asked Muhammad. Who is *she*? He looked at me, startled. My wife, he said. Mayya.

I heard a faint laugh coming from the back seat. Suppressed and derisive, it was a laugh I knew very well. I brought my arm in from the car window and said without turning around, Don't laugh at me, Papa. You aren't even here any more. You died the year Muhammad was born. The laugh only grew louder and in the car mirror I saw my father's white beard shaking.

Salim passed by the car window, running, followed by two young fellows, but older than he was, chasing him in a Porsche. I turned toward Muhammad but I found London, crying. Yes, Papa, she said. I am successful, yes. Muhammad was a baby in her lap, shaking his head hard in one of those endless jerky movements he always made. The car faded away and Muhammad and I were sitting on the beach. Muhammad looked like a totally ordinary strapping young man. He was whistling happily, and suddenly he said to me, I can't stand it any more, Abdallah, her jealousy will kill me. I turned to him. Who is she? Who do you mean? My wife, he said. I grabbed the sleeve of his grey dishdasha. But you are still little, and you are sick, and you do not have a wife.

He screamed. My wife will kill me! She keeps her eyes on my phone, she surrounds me. He collapsed, still shouting. She is always bent over that damned sewing machine, she strokes it, but she never once bends over me. The saliva began to drip from his mouth as his hand made those repeated sharp nervous movements. I slapped him, saying over and over, Shut up, you're making a scene, you're scandalizing us.

My father snatched the whip from my hands. He threw it into the sea. But you are dead, Papa, I said to him. How can you come back like this?

He went away, not turning back once. I shouted after him. Take him with you, Papa! Take Muhammad with you.

Everything went dark. I heard the sound of my car starting, I heard it leaving. I caught a glimpse of London at the wheel. I scooped Muhammad into my arms. He is like a fish, Muhammad is, I suddenly thought. I walked down to the water. The waves were welling up, and I went in up to my chest. When I opened my arms Muhammad slipped away like a fish. And I came out of the water dry.